"Trent?" ~~Annie's~~ **suddenly** ~~dry.~~

His gaze was focused on her mouth. "I'm trying to talk myself out of kissing you. It might help if you would push me away or something."

She lifted a hand to his chest, but it simply rested there, feeling his heart beating strongly against her palm. "I should push you away," she murmured, trying to convince herself.

"Yes." His other hand rose, cupping her face. His head lowered until his mouth almost, but not quite, touched hers.

Impulsively, Annie tightened her fingers around the fabric of his shirt and closed the distance between them. She had come to Honoria to make her own decisions. To try new experiences. And she had just decided that kissing Trent McBride was an experience she didn't want to miss. So, before she lost her nerve, she touched her lips to his.

She might have taken the initiative, but Trent quickly turned that around. He gathered her in his arms and transformed her tentative kiss into an embrace that nearly singed her eyelashes.

She should have known, she thought, wrapping her arms around his neck, that Trent McBride would kiss like this....

Dear Reader,

With every book I write, I start with the question "What if?" What if a man who was born to fly becomes permanently grounded by a tragic accident? What if this man, who no longer considers himself hero material, falls in love with a woman who seems to be in need of one?

These were the questions I asked myself when I began writing *Secretly Yours*, the second book about those Wild McBrides. Luckily, Trent and I discovered together that he is still more than "wild" enough to be the perfect hero for Annie Stewart, the young woman who's come to Honoria, Georgia, to start a new life. And it's a good thing, because Annie's going to need a hero when her old life catches up with her....

What no one in Honoria knows is that there's still one member of the McBride family they haven't met—and this one could be the "wildest" McBride of them all. Mac Cordero's whole life has been a scandal. He's coming to town for answers—and a taste of revenge. Don't miss Mac's story in *Yesterday's Scandal*, a Harlequin single title, on sale September 2000.

Enjoy,

Gina Wilkins

Books by Gina Wilkins

HARLEQUIN TEMPTATION
749—THE LITTLEST STOWAWAY
792—SEDUCTIVELY YOURS*

*The Wild McBrides

Gina Wilkins
SECRETLY YOURS

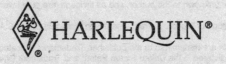

HARLEQUIN®

TORONTO • NEW YORK • LONDON
AMSTERDAM • PARIS • SYDNEY • HAMBURG
STOCKHOLM • ATHENS • TOKYO • MILAN • MADRID
PRAGUE • WARSAW • BUDAPEST • AUCKLAND

For my sisters-in-law: Lisa, Sandy and LuLu, who
love to remind me that they're younger than I am.

ISBN 0-373-25896-8

SECRETLY YOURS

Visit us at www.eHarlequin.com

Printed in U.S.A.

1

"YOU'VE DONE *WHAT?*" Trent McBride asked, in a voice that had been known to make his peers quake.

But Bobbie McBride had never been easily intimidated—and especially not by one of her own three offspring. She faced her youngest without flinching. "I've hired a housekeeper for you. You've heard us mention Annie Stewart, who's been cleaning the McBride Law Firm offices since she moved to town six weeks ago. She's very conscientious and she's already got quite a few clients, but she still needs steady work."

"I don't need a housekeeper."

"You most certainly do. You keep this place tidy enough, I'll admit, but Annie will take care of the little details you never even notice. She'll do your laundry, too."

"I can wash my own underwear."

His mother continued as if she hadn't heard him. "She'll come twice a week, on Tuesdays and Fridays, and stay a couple of hours each time. I've arranged to have her start next week."

Though he, better than most, knew the futility of trying to argue with his mother, Trent made the effort, anyway. "I don't want her to start next week. How am I supposed to pay a housekeeper on what's left of my insurance settlement? And before you even suggest it, I'm not letting you and Dad pay for this."

"You never let us pay for *anything*," Bobbie replied matter-of-factly. "All three of my children are stubborn as mules and irritatingly independent. But you, my dear Trent, have always taken first place. As it happens, I've worked out all the details regarding payment, too. I'm sure you've heard that Annie moved into the old Stewart place just down the road from here. Turns out strange old Carney Stewart was her great-uncle, and he left the house and property to her when he died last year. No one even knew Carney *had* family until then. Anyway, the place is in terrible shape, and it needs a lot of repairs. I told Annie you're a skilled woodworker, and she's willing to trade her services in exchange for yours."

"I am not a handyman."

"Perhaps not, but you're certainly available. And it will be good for you to get out of the house more. As long as you're reasonably careful, the exercise will be good for you, too. Not to mention the fact that you'll be doing a big favor to a very nice young woman."

"I don't do favors."

"You'll do this one." Her voice was as soft as his—and just as unyielding.

Bobbie McBride had been a schoolteacher for more than thirty years. When she got started on one of her famous lectures, there was no stopping her. And when that lecture was directed toward one of her three adult children, there was no point in trying to interrupt. Though Trent had recently turned twenty-six, his mother could still reduce him to a sullen adolescent.

"If you think for one minute that I'm going to let you live out the rest of your life brooding in this cottage like some sort of crusty old hermit, you are very mistaken," she said flatly. "Do you want to end up like Carney Stewart, old and alone? I've given you more than a year to pull yourself together. It's been eighteen months since the accident. It's time for you to stop sulking and get on with your life."

Trent kept his gaze focused on the unadorned wall in front of him. "I'm not sulking. I'm living exactly the way I choose."

"You sit here alone for days. You rarely go out in public. You neglect your family and rebuff your friends. You aren't eating right and you aren't doing the exercises you were given. *This* is the way you choose to live?"

"Yes," he answered simply.

She shook her gray head in exasperation. "Well, I'm not going to stand by quietly while you ruin your life."

"Too late, Mother." He tried to sound bored, but he was aware of the undertones of self-pity. "I did that eighteen months ago."

"Sometimes," she said after a moment, "what I think you need most is to be taken behind the woodshed."

He was surprised to feel one corner of his mouth twitch in what was almost a smile. "You just might be right."

Bobbie reached for her coat. "I have to be going. Annie will be here Tuesday morning at nine. You two can work out the details of this arrangement then."

As tempted as he was to refuse, he knew it wouldn't

be worth the effort. "All right. I'll give it a month, but that's it, Mother."

Satisfied with her limited victory, Bobbie allowed him to usher her out of his house. Closing the door behind her, Trent growled and shoved a hand through his shaggy blond hair—his usual reaction to a visit from his mother. Now what had she gotten him into?

IT WAS A GLOOMY February morning, windy and gray, the heavy clouds overhead threatening a cold winter rain. Looking from the glowering sky to the darkened cottage in front of her, Annie Stewart tried to decide which seemed the most sinister.

She almost chose to risk the elements. Judging from the whispers she'd heard about Trent McBride during the past six weeks, she wasn't at all sure what she would find inside his cottage.

Rumor had it that he'd been injured in a plane crash—one he had barely survived. They said the crash had left him scarred, physically and emotionally. He'd changed, they whispered, from the town's golden boy to an angry, withdrawn hermit. Martha Godwin, one of Annie's new clients who was known as the town's primary source of inside information, had hinted that Trent hadn't been "quite right" since the accident.

"Sits in that house out in the woods all by himself," she had elaborated darkly. "Doesn't go anywhere, doesn't see anyone but family. Every time I ask his parents about him, they just shake their heads. There were plenty of local single women who were more than willing to nurse him back to health. Heck, there was a regular parade of them trotting out to his place with casseroles and silly smiles, but he sent them all packing. I tried to visit him once myself—just to be neighborly—but he wouldn't let me in. Said he was busy, though I can't imagine what he was doing."

Since Annie had experience with Martha's relentless prying, having fielded quite a few personal questions of her own, she didn't blame the guy. But it did seem strange to her that a young man, not even thirty yet, would isolate himself from everyone this way.

Reaching his front door, she looked for a doorbell, but didn't see one. Her hand was actually shaking when she lifted it to knock. She sighed in exasperation. What was wrong with her today? Why did she have this weird feeling that her life was going to change when she knocked on this door? She had made a lot of changes during the past couple of months. How hard could it be to add a new name to her growing client list—even if she had been warned that this client was different?

Gathering her courage, and castigating herself for her cowardice, she knocked. She was being ridiculous to let her imagination run away with her this way. Whatever Trent McBride's problems, this was hardly a scene from *Beauty and the Beast*. For one thing, she didn't consider herself any great beauty. And Trent might be wounded, but he certainly wasn't a beast.

She knew his family, and they were all nice, normal people. How different could he be?

She knocked again, thinking perhaps he hadn't heard her first timid effort. After another moment, the door opened.

A man she assumed to be Trent McBride stood in

the shadows inside the darkened house, so that she couldn't quite make out his features. She could see that he was tall—around six feet—and thin, perhaps a bit too thin. Blond, she decided, catching a glimmer of gold in the shadows. "Mr. McBride?"

"You're the housekeeper?" His voice was deep, and slightly rough.

Though it still felt strange to hear herself identified that way, Annie answered simply, "Yes. I'm Annie Stewart."

After another pause, he stepped out of the doorway. "Come in."

When she instinctively hesitated, he reached out to snap on the overhead light. The cavelike room was instantly transformed into a more welcoming environment. The few pieces of furniture were very nice, she noted as she walked slowly inside, but the room had a spartan air to it. Even motel rooms had more personality.

Having procrastinated as long as she could, she turned to face Trent. She thought she had prepared herself for anything—scars, disfigurement, whatever evidence a plane crash might have left. She certainly hadn't expected to be facing sheer masculine perfection.

Thick golden hair framed a face that Annie suspected had received more than its fair share of feminine attention. No wonder so many local women had been anxious to visit him after his accident. Behind the lenses of a pair of gold-tone metal glasses, his eyes were very blue. If he ever smiled—which she saw no evidence of at that moment—she imagined that his angled cheeks would crease appealingly. Whatever damage his accident had caused—and Martha Godwin had led her to believe it was extensive—it certainly hadn't been done to his face.

If they *had* been playing a scene from *Beauty and the Beast*, she thought wryly, she suspected she knew who would be cast as the beauty—and it wasn't her.

"You're younger than I expected," he said, studying her with an intensity that unnerved her.

You're prettier than I expected, she would have liked to respond, but that sort of flipness didn't fit her new position. "Is that a problem?" she asked instead.

He shrugged. "My mother said you need some repairs done."

"Yes. My great-uncle's house was in worse shape than I thought when I first moved in, and I'm afraid I can't afford a lot of improvements just yet. She suggested that you could take care of some of the most pressing problems while I work for you, and I told her it seemed a fair trade, if you're agreeable."

She couldn't help noticing that he didn't look overly enthused by the arrangement, but he nodded. "I'll head over to your place now. Anything you want done there first?"

"I'd really appreciate it if you could fix the front step," she answered tentatively. "I've almost tripped a couple of times because it's loose. I tried to stabilize it, but I'm afraid I'm not very good with that sort of thing."

Another nod. "Do whatever you want around here—dust, vacuum, fluff—but don't rearrange the furniture. I like everything where it is."

She almost imitated him and nodded. Resisting, she said instead, "Of course. Any other instructions?"

"No." He turned and moved toward the door, apparently intending to leave without another word.

She felt as though she should say something. "Mr. McBride?"

He glanced over his shoulder, looking impatient. "What?"

"If you need to go inside my house, there's a key hidden beneath the big rock beside the front step."

She certainly wasn't surprised that his only response was a nod.

"Definitely an odd man," she murmured when the front door had closed behind him. By the time she went out to her car to collect her cleaning supplies, both he and the old truck that had been parked outside when she'd arrived were gone. Carrying her things into his house, she found herself comparing him to the other McBrides she had met.

The McBride Law Firm had been one of her first clients, one she'd found only days after she'd arrived in town. Trent's brother, Trevor, the man who'd hired her after a brief interview, was polished, charming, personable. Their father, Caleb, the senior partner of the firm, was the personification of a soft-spoken, good-humored Southern lawyer. It was through that custodial job that Annie had met Trent's mother, Bobbie, who was talkative, well-intentioned and seemed to have an almost compulsive need to take care of everyone around her.

From her first impression, it was hard to believe Trent was related to any of the McBrides.

Not that she really cared whether he was unfriendly

or even downright surly, she assured herself. Her only interest in Trent was that he had agreed—whether willingly or not—to do some much-needed repairs on her house in exchange for her cleaning his. A fair trade of services, no personal relationship implied. Which was exactly the way she wanted it to remain. Annie had no interest in forming a personal relationship with *anyone* in Honoria, Georgia, for now. After her recent debacle of an engagement, she certainly wasn't interested in getting involved with another man for a while—especially one as difficult as Trent McBride seemed to be.

Even if he *was* gorgeous.

She pulled a spray bottle of kitchen cleaner out of her supplies and started to work on Trent McBride's already-neat kitchen. No one would ever claim that Annie Stewart didn't fully earn her pay.

THOUGH HE HADN'T SEEN it in years, the old Stewart place was in even worse shape than Trent had remembered. Even the lot had gotten smaller as the surrounding woods had been allowed to encroach on what had once been a decent-size yard. It wasn't a bad house—good, solid structure overall—but it had been allowed to deteriorate before old Stewart had died, and had been vacant for almost a year since. The place needed a lot more than he could do in a month, he decided, pushing his glasses up on his nose, but he could at least make it reasonably safe for its present occupant.

Okay, maybe he had been a little bored lately—though he wouldn't have admitted it to his mother for any reason.

Remembering what Annie had said about the front step, he set his toolbox beside it. He noted immediately that the step was not only broken, it was actually dangerous. It was a wonder Annie hadn't fallen, landing on the oversize rocks that had been used to outline the unplanted flower beds on either side of the front door. He frowned as he recalled her saying that she'd almost tripped several times. She was very lucky she hadn't.

Pulling out a hammer, a handful of nails and a level, he found himself thinking about Annie Stewart. She hadn't been at all what he'd expected. For some reason, he thought she'd be older—much older. But she'd looked even younger than his own twenty-six years—and was so small and delicate he could hardly imagine her tackling heavy cleaning every day.

He supposed she could be considered pretty—if he had a taste for a heart-shaped face dominated by big, long-lashed brown eyes. Or a tip-tilted nose and a full, soft mouth bracketed by shallow dimples. Add to those attributes her glossy, shoulder-length, chestnut-brown hair and a petite, but definitely feminine figure, and most men would probably start fantasizing about getting to know her better. Trent, on the other hand, had taken one look at her and made a silent vow to keep his distance.

If there was one thing he *didn't* need in his life now, it was a sweet young thing who seemed to be in even worse shape than he was, judging from what his mother had told him. Annie apparently had no family, no friends in town yet and obviously no money if she was forced to live in this dump. He, on the other hand, had more family than he knew what to do with, old friends who were determined to stay involved in his life even though he had tried his best to push them away, and a nagging uncertainty about his future that seemed to have no workable solution.

He definitely had no interest in getting involved in Annie Stewart's problems—whatever they were. He would make this house reasonably safe for her to live in—at least as much as he could accomplish in the four weeks he'd granted her—and then he would sequester himself into his own sanctuary again. No matter how hard his mother and others tried to drag him out.

BY THE TIME Annie finished cleaning Trent's place, she was in love—with his furniture. Polishing his wood was the most sensual experience she'd had in ages, she thought ironically, slowly stroking a hand over a satiny-smooth cherry tabletop.

The solid wood, raised panel cabinets in his kitchen were works of art. The tables and chairs were solid, exquisitely crafted and so beautiful she found herself wasting several minutes just admiring them. An oversize rocker beside the stone fireplace in his cozy living room proved an irresistible temptation; she was unable to deny herself the pleasure of sinking into it, putting her head back and slowly rocking for ten blissfully lazy minutes.

The hand-crafted furniture was the only evidence of personality she found anywhere in Trent's four-room cottage.

Bobbie McBride had claimed her son was a skilled woodworker. If these pieces were examples of his work, Bobbie had been guilty of major understatement.

Before she left, she wrote Trent a note and stuck it to the refrigerator with a magnet. It was simple and to the point: "Mr. McBride, the lightbulb in the bedroom blew out. I don't know where you keep the replacement bulbs." She wasn't able to resist adding, "Your furniture is beautiful."

Long after she left his house, while she was cleaning and scrubbing other places, Annie regretted that impulsive postscript. He'd made it clear he wanted to keep their arrangement strictly professional. She wouldn't be the one to cross that line again.

THE FIRST THING Trent noticed when he limped into his house four hours after he'd left Annie there was the faint, fresh scent of lemon. It smelled clean, he thought.

The scent reminded him of Saturday afternoons from his childhood; his mother had spent nearly every Saturday morning cleaning and polishing. Because he didn't like to dwell on the carefree days of his youth, days he wouldn't see again, he pushed the memories away and headed for the kitchen in search of a cold drink and a pain pill. His back ached, letting him know he'd done too much today. He hated being nagged—even by his own abused body.

He spotted Annie's note as soon as he entered the room. Prissy handwriting, he thought, deciding it looked like her. He could still hear the prim, polite way she'd called him "Mr. McBride." He read the note, his attention lingering on the last line.

She thought his furniture was beautiful. Had she guessed that he'd made most of it himself? Had she somehow known that his woodworking was the only thing he took any pride or satisfaction from these days? It annoyed him that her compliment pleased him.

Scowling, he pulled the note from the refrigerator and tossed it into the trash.

ANNIE CLEANED the McBride Law Firm offices three afternoons a week—Mondays, Wednesdays, and Fridays. She usually arrived just as everyone else was leaving and then locked up when she finished. She was running a bit late on Wednesday, the day after she'd cleaned Trent's house, and everyone was already gone except Trevor McBride, who was working late in his office behind a pile of papers. A still-steaming mug of coffee sat at his elbow. Photos of his wife and his two young children lined the credenza behind him, giving a sweetly personal touch to the otherwise ultraprofessional office.

He looked up with a smile when she entered. "Hello, Annie. How are you?"

"Fine, thank you, Mr. McBride." She pushed a limp, damp strand of hair away from her face and returned the smile ruefully. "Except for resembling a drowned rat, of course. It's really pouring out there."

He cocked his head, listening to the rain hitting the windows. "So I hear. It doesn't seem to be letting up."

"I hope it stops before I get home. The way my bedroom roof leaks, I'd hate to drown in my sleep," she said with a wry smile.

"Would you like some coffee? I just made a fresh pot."

"No, thank you." Having left her wet raincoat in the rest room off the lobby, Annie felt confident that she wasn't dripping on the carpet when she crossed the room to empty his wastebasket. "I'll be working in the other rooms. Let me know when you're ready for me to clean in here."

"All right. By the way..."

She paused in the doorway, studying him. Blond and blue-eyed like his younger brother, Trevor was an attractive man, though perhaps not as breathtakingly spectacular as Trent—at least in Annie's opinion. She imagined his wife would probably disagree about which McBride brother was the most appealing. "Yes?"

He seemed to choose his words carefully. "Mother told me about the service-swapping deal she made between you and Trent. That's a satisfactory arrangement for you? You didn't let my mother railroad you into it, I hope."

She smiled. "It's a very satisfactory arrangement for me. I actually feel as though I'm getting the better end of the bargain. Your brother's house is small, and he keeps it very neat. It definitely doesn't need much cleaning. But he worked very hard at my place yesterday. I couldn't believe how much he'd gotten done in just one morning."

Trent had repaired her precarious front step, replaced a broken board on the small porch and tightened a shutter that had hung loose at one window. He'd even mended the screen door, which had previously hung crookedly from a broken hinge.

"Trent needs something to do to get him out of the rut he's got himself into," Trevor said. "This will be good for him."

"I don't know about that, but it's certainly helpful to me. It's really sweet of your brother to do this."

Trevor choked on a sip of coffee. "Sweet?" he repeated, recovering his voice. "Trent? Er...have you actually met him, by any chance?"

"Only briefly, yesterday morning."

"And you thought he was, um, sweet?"

"I said what he's doing is sweet," she corrected, hesitant to apply the word to Trent, himself. "Helping me with the repairs, I mean."

"I see." He chuckled.

"What's so funny?"

"Prior to his accident, I heard my brother referred to as wild, cocky and reckless. During the past year or so he's been called sullen, surly and rude. I'm not sure anyone has *ever* called him 'sweet.'"

Though she was intrigued, Annie didn't think she should be gossiping about one of her clients, even with his brother. "Still, I appreciate having my front step fixed so I won't break my neck. Now, if you'll excuse me, I have a job to do."

She heard him laughing softly behind her when she left his office. It seemed that Trent wasn't the only odd brother in the McBride family, she thought with a bemused shake of her head.

TRENT WAS in his workshop Thursday night, rubbing wood stain onto a newly finished shelf, when the cellular telephone he'd brought in with him rang. He glared at the intrusive instrument, wishing he could simply ignore it, but it was probably his mother. If he didn't answer, she would come charging over to find out what was wrong. He lifted the receiver to his ear. "What?"

"Hello to you, too," Trevor said, apparently amused rather than offended by his younger brother's curtness.

"What do you want, Trevor? I'm busy."

"I'm fine, thanks, and so are the wife and kids. Nice of you to ask."

"If you only called to needle me..."

"No, wait. Don't hang up. I really do have a reason for calling."

"Well?"

"Jamie wants you to come to dinner tomorrow evening. She's trying out a new recipe for gumbo."

Trevor swallowed a sigh. He didn't want to hurt his sister-in-law's feelings, but he really hadn't been in the mood lately for cozy family dinners. He'd made that clear enough to his relatives, and they generally respected his wishes, but every so often they felt compelled to drag him out again. He understood, sort of, but he wished they could just accept his need for more time and space to come to terms with what had happened to him. "All right. I'll come."

"Try to contain your enthusiasm, will you?"

"Is there anything else you want?" Trent asked pointedly.

"No, but it was 'sweet' of you to ask. Of course, I've been told recently that you're a very 'sweet' man."

"Who the hell told you that?" he asked, startled.

Trevor laughed. "Your housekeeper. Apparently, you've earned her undying gratitude by fixing her front step."

"It's a wonder she hasn't broken a leg on it—or worse," Trent muttered.

"Pretty, isn't she? Intriguing, too. I haven't figured her out yet."

"You shouldn't be trying. You're a married man."

"Mmm. But *you're* not."

"Forget it. Not interested."

"Then you're even more of a cretin than I gave you credit for."

"Goodbye, Trevor."

"One more thing," his brother said quickly, hearing the finality in Trent's tone. "Annie mentioned that her roof is leaking. You might want to look into it, but don't take any unnecessary risks. If you need help, give me a call and I'll—"

"I'll take care of it."

"All right. We'll expect you for dinner tomorrow."

"I'll be there," Trent grumbled, then hung up before his brother could prolong the conversation.

Pushing the lid onto the can of stain, he considered what he knew about Annie Stewart. She thought he was sweet. And she liked his furniture. And something about her shy smile made his stomach muscles quiver, damn it.

This was going to be a long month.

2

ANNIE wore a briskly professional smile when Trent opened his door to her on Friday morning. The smile momentarily wavered when she saw him. As she'd left her house that morning, oddly nervous about seeing him again, she had tried to convince herself that he couldn't really be as gorgeous as she'd remembered. But he was—and then some.

Not that his attractiveness should make any difference to her, of course. She was here to do a job, not to drool over her client. "Good morning, Mr. McBride."

He seemed to study her smile for a moment, then nodded and reached out to relieve her of her supplies. Without speaking, he held the door so she could enter with her lightweight vacuum cleaner.

She had to pass within inches of him to step inside, which made her even more aware of his height and the intriguing width of his shoulders. Chiding herself for being so easily and so uncharacteristically distracted from the job at hand, she asked, "Is there anything in particular you want me to do here today?"

He shrugged. "Whatever needs doing. I heard your roof is leaking. How bad is it?"

She frowned. "How did you... Oh, you've talked with your brother."

"Yes. So, where's the leak?"

Unsure how she felt about knowing he and Trevor had been talking about her, even in passing, she replied, "The worst leak is in my bedroom, but there's also a small drip in the kitchen."

"I'll look into it."

"If there are any supplies you need, I'll pay for them, of course."

He nodded. "I get a discount at the local hardware store. If I need anything, I'll put it on my account there and you can reimburse me."

She hoped the supplies wouldn't be too expensive. The money she'd brought with her to Honoria had been severely depleted by utility deposits and other expenses required to move into the run-down house she'd inherited from her eccentric great-uncle. She still had money in her savings account from the sale last year of her uncle's possessions, but she wanted to spend it wisely. Until she built a more solid clientele for her cleaning service, her income was somewhat limited.

She thought wistfully of the bank account she had in Atlanta, money she wouldn't touch unless it was absolutely necessary. After ending an engagement that had been the worst mistake of her life, she had boldly declared her independence from her family and their money nearly two months ago during a blazing row with her overbearing father. It had been her twenty-sixth birthday, and she had announced that she was quite capable of taking care of herself, paying her own bills, making her own decisions. She only wished she had known just how daunting—and expensive—such a declaration would be.

The money wouldn't have made any difference, she

assured herself, still convinced she'd made the right decision. But at least a little forewarning would have kept her from being so overwhelmed by the financial reality of owning an old, neglected house.

Realizing that Trent was studying her intently, and that she must have been standing there frowning for several long moments, she smoothed her expression. "Thank you all the work you've done, and especially for fixing my step. I feel much safer on it now."

He answered in a growl. "It was an accident waiting to happen. You're lucky you haven't broken your neck."

"You're sure there's nothing special you want me to do here today?"

She was beginning to think he wasn't going to answer when he surprised her by saying, "I'm out of clean socks. You can do a load of laundry, if you have time."

She smiled, pleased that he'd made a request for a change. "Sure. No problem."

"Lock up when you leave," he said, turning abruptly away.

"Yes, I will. And Mr. McBride, I—"

Whatever she might have said faded into silence when he left without another word. He was walking stiffly today, she noted. Had he hurt himself working at her place Tuesday? She couldn't help worrying about those injuries Martha Godwin had hinted at, but she suspected Trent wouldn't appreciate personal questions.

Since she was no more interested in answering personal questions than he probably was, she decided she had better just mind her own business.

IT HAD BEEN a long time since Trent had been drawn out of his own problems enough to be actively curious about anyone else. But as he sat on Annie Stewart's roof, pounding nails into loose shingles, he found himself wondering about her. He knew why *he* had chosen to live a hermit's life during the past year—mostly because he hadn't known what else to do—but what was Annie's story? What had brought her to Honoria? Where was her family?

She seemed intelligent enough and he would be willing to bet she was well educated. So why had she chosen to clean houses for a living? Had she no other goals, no plans? No dreams?

Had her dreams, like his, been taken away, leaving her lost and aimless—a condition he knew all too well?

"I had a feeling I would find you up there."

Frowning, Trent pushed his glasses higher on his nose and looked over the edge of the roof. His brother stood on the ground below, his hands on his hips as he gazed upward. "You should know better than to sneak up on a guy who's alone on a roof."

"And you should know better than to *be* alone on a roof. You want to risk ending up in a wheelchair again?"

Trent hated being reminded of his limitations. "You're the one who told me Annie's roof leaked. I'm fixing it."

"I also told you I would help you." Trevor planted a foot on the bottom rung of the ladder propped against the side of the house.

Trent suddenly realized that his brother wore jeans

and a sweatshirt rather than his usual suit and tie. "Don't you have to work today?"

Joining him on the roof, Trevor shook his head. "Nope. I took the day off. Mental-health day. I don't have to be in court, and all my appointments can wait until next week. Jamie's teaching, Sam's in school and Abbie's with the nanny. Today is all mine."

"So you decided to spend it on Annie's roof."

Trevor shrugged and reached for an extra hammer from Trent's toolbox. "I decided to spend it with you."

Trent had to make an effort to grumble. "I'm having dinner at your house this evening. Isn't that enough family togetherness for you?"

Unoffended, Trevor moved to a curled shingle and examined it. "The roof really needs to be replaced altogether."

Remembering Annie's cautious look when she'd offered to reimburse him for supplies, Trent shrugged. "I don't think she can afford that right now. I'm patching the leaks as well as possible until she can have the whole job done."

Trevor reached for a handful of roofing nails. "Having any trouble with your back?"

His back ached every time he stretched and bent, actually, but he had gotten used to pain. On a scale of one to ten—and he was all too well acquainted with ten—he considered his current discomfort a six. "I'm fine."

"Good. Just be careful not to overdo it."

"Now you're starting to sound like Mom."

Trevor made a production of looking horrified. "God forbid."

A small plane passed overhead, flying low as it

headed for the private airstrip on the north side of town. Trent's gaze was involuntarily drawn upward. He noted automatically that the craft was a Beechcraft V-tail, that the landing gear was already down, the descent slow and smooth. His knuckles tightened around his hammer, and he could almost feel the yoke in his hands.

The plane disappeared behind a line of trees. His memories flashed to the last time he'd flown. And then moved further ahead, images so vivid he could almost smell the smoke again, hear the creak and pop of heating metal, feel the pain of his injuries and the sick certainty that he would die there in the wreckage of aircraft and ego, a casualty of his own recklessness.

"Trent?"

Something in his brother's voice made Trent suspect it wasn't the first time he'd spoken. "What?"

"Are you okay?"

"Are you going to talk or nail shingles?" Trent retorted, chagrined at being caught in one of his frequent daytime nightmares. The ones during the night were even worse, but at least he had no witnesses then.

Trevor sighed and moved to a new spot. "Forgive me for being concerned," he muttered.

Pointedly ignoring him, Trent went back to work, concentrating fiercely on the task and pushing the memories to the back of his mind.

THERE WAS ANOTHER NOTE on Trent's refrigerator when he arrived home that afternoon. "Your laundry is folded on the bed," it read. "I didn't know if you wanted me to open closets and drawers to put things away. I forgot to ask."

Again, there was a postscript: "Did you make that big rocker by the fireplace? It's fabulous."

Shaking his head, Trent reached into the fridge and pulled out a cola. He drained a third of it in one long guzzle, then read the note in his hand again. Annie seemed to have a thing for his furniture.

Remembering the worn odds and ends of furniture he'd seen when he went in her house to check the ceiling for signs of leaks, he suspected that most of it had been chosen for economy rather than personal taste.

She was definitely an odd cookie, he thought, tossing the note onto the counter. Pretty, but odd.

He moved into his bedroom to put his neatly folded socks and underwear away, and found himself wondering again what her story was. It irritated him to realize that he was suddenly feeling rather protective of her. Working on her roof earlier, he'd had the irritatingly satisfying feeling that he was helping someone who needed him.

As if he had anything to offer Annie—or anyone, he added with a heavy scowl.

THE FIRST THING Annie always did when she returned home on Tuesday and Friday afternoons was to find out what Trent had done that day. It amazed her how much he had accomplished in the three weeks that had passed since they had begun their arrangement. Their only personal interaction during those weeks had been the mornings when she arrived at his house to clean.

She thought she'd done a decent job of hiding her

reaction to him during those fleeting encounters. She wanted to think he had no idea that she all but melted every time he looked at her in that sizzlingly intense manner of his. But she wouldn't be surprised if he suspected it, anyway. A man like Trent had to be used to finding puddles of women at his feet.

His mother had warned her that Trent considered their arrangement only temporary and was likely to end it at any time, but Annie wasn't worried. Even if he decided today that they'd swapped their last service, she still believed it had been well worth it. Her front step was safe to walk on now, her roof hadn't leaked during a fairly heavy rain yesterday, he had cleaned out her gutters and unclogged her drains. She didn't know how many hours he'd spent there—he was always gone by the time she came home—but she knew he'd spent more time working at her place than she had at his.

Determined to repay him, she had worked very hard at his place—cleaning, scrubbing, shining and polishing everything in his house. He'd given her free rein, so she had scrubbed floors, cleaned the oven and refrigerator and washed windows—inside and out. She'd dusted and vacuumed everything that hadn't moved, but it still didn't feel like enough.

There was an odd intimacy to spending so much time in his home while he was working in hers. She didn't feel that way about her other clients, seeing their houses as just rooms to clean and money to earn—but it was different, somehow, with Trent. She told herself it was only because she was aware that he was as familiar with her home as she was with his.

There was certainly no more personal element involved between them.

When she walked into her place on the first Tuesday afternoon in March—her fourth week of working for Trent—she was startled to find his big wooden rocker sitting in her living room. No, not *his* rocker, she realized, taking a step closer. Just as beautiful, but not the same. The color was slightly different, the grain not quite like the other.

There was a note taped to the back of the chair. In printed block letters it said, "You said you like my rocker. This was the first one I made. I broke the arm and had to glue it, but if you want it, it's yours." He hadn't bothered to sign his name.

Her heart in her throat, she studied the rocker more closely. She found the break he'd referred to, eventually. The wood had apparently split when he'd nailed it, but he'd repaired it so expertly that only an obsessive perfectionist could find fault with it. But she was crazy about it, trivial flaw and all.

Hardly able to believe what he had done, she sank into the chair and began to rock, her work-weary muscles almost sighing in relief. Annie had grown up surrounded by beautiful, expensive things, but she had never fallen this hard for any inanimate object.

She could picture herself sitting in this wonderful chair on the cold nights still ahead, rocking, resting, listening to music from the stereo she was going to buy as soon as she had saved enough. Everything her uncle had owned had been sold at an estate auction, by his request, a few months after he'd died, and the proceeds had been deposited into an account for her, so there had been no furniture when she'd moved into the house he'd left her. She'd had to pick up a few odds and ends at secondhand shops to get by until she could do better. This chair was now the nicest piece she possessed. Having this beautiful rocker to relax in would certainly brighten up her evenings.

She had never envisioned herself living alone this way, but there were times when she actually enjoyed it enough to forget about the loneliness.

Had her uncle Carney enjoyed the solitary existence he'd led here? Eccentric and free-spirited, he'd rebelled early against the stringent expectations of his family—something Annie now understood all too well. She hadn't seen her uncle often, only when he breezed through Atlanta to make contact with his only living relatives—her father and her—a total of only half a dozen times or so that Annie could remember. But he had always seemed fond of her, telling her wonderful stories about all the places he had seen, all the adventures he'd had.

He'd settled in Honoria—for reasons no one but him had ever known—after he'd broken a hip and had no longer been able to travel as he once had. He'd lived here nearly ten years before his death, but apparently hadn't really gotten to know anyone in this town very well. Annie hoped to make a few more friends here than her great-uncle had. She only wished that she could have gotten to know Carney, himself, better. He would have understood, as no one else could, her need to break away from her parents, her father, in particular.

Her hand still stroking the chair, she glanced at the telephone nearby. Trent wasn't the type to graciously accept gratitude—he'd always brushed her off when she'd tried to thank him for the work he'd done here—but she couldn't wait until Friday to tell him how much this meant to her.

He answered in his usual curt manner. "H'lo?"

She spoke without bothering to identify herself. "Thank you. The chair is beautiful."

"You didn't have to call. I said you can have it if you want it."

"Of course I want it. I love it. But—"

"Good. It was in my way here. I don't need two."

"I'd like to pay you for it," she offered boldly. "You must have spent hours making it. Not to mention the materials."

"Forget it. It wasn't for sale, anyway. I told you, it's flawed."

"But—"

"Look, do you want the chair or not?"

She sighed. "Yes."

"Fine. Enjoy it. See you Friday."

A dial tone sounded in her ear before she could say anything else.

Blinking, she hung up the receiver, then laughed incredulously, shaking her head. Trent McBride was one of the most exasperating men she had ever met. Rude, moody, withdrawn—and yet there was a streak of kindness and generosity in him that he hadn't quite been able to hide from her.

She had learned a little more about him during the past three weeks. She hadn't asked questions—she would consider that both unprofessional and unethical—but the people here seemed anxious to volunteer information about each other. They'd told her that Trent had been hospitalized for weeks after his accident, and that his injuries, whatever they were, had put an end to his air force career. And now everyone wondered what he was going to do with the rest of his life.

Annie wondered about that herself—not that it was any of her business, of course. Several of her clients had tried to pump her for information about Trent, but she refused to cooperate, skillfully changing the subject whenever his name came up.

She crossed the room, stroked a hand over one satiny-smooth arm of the rocker, then sank into it again. Putting her head back, she closed her eyes and began to rock. The pleasurable sigh that escaped her seemed to echo in the quiet room.

GIVING ANNIE THE CHAIR had probably been a mistake, Trent thought glumly as he stared into his refrigerator on Friday of the following week. He'd thought she might like it, but he hadn't been prepared for her to show her gratitude quite so...fervently. A stack of casserole dishes—enough for several days of meals—were neatly stacked in the fridge. Two loaves of fresh-baked bread sat on his counter. There was a plant on his kitchen windowsill, for Pete's sake.

He'd only given her an extra chair that had been sitting in his workshop—a chair with a patched arm, for that matter. Had no one ever been nice to the woman before? He should have tried harder to talk himself out of the impulse when it had first occurred to him.

He closed the refrigerator and reached for the cup of coffee he'd poured a few minutes earlier. He'd thought he was hungry, but seeing all that food in there had killed his appetite. No more generous gestures, he promised himself. He didn't want to encourage any more awkward expressions of gratitude.

She knocked on his front door just as he finished his coffee. As he went to let her in, he hoped she wasn't bringing food or flowers this time.

Fortunately she was only carrying her cleaning supplies. She gave him one of her dimpled smiles when he reached out to relieve her of the heavy tote. He hated the way his abdomen tightened when she did that.

He was trying his best not to be attracted to her. But he was. He didn't even particularly want to like her. But he did. Damn it.

"Good morning," she said.

He nodded, dragging his gaze away from her sweetly curved mouth. "I thought I would fix that kitchen-cabinet door by your sink today. I noticed it keeps swinging open."

Her smile tilted ruefully. "I can't tell you how many times I've hit my head on it. I was beginning to think I was going to have a permanent goose egg on my forehead."

He glanced automatically at her smooth forehead, seeing no damage there. No flaws at all, for that matter.

"Anything special you want me to do here?" she asked, her voice suddenly uncertain—as if the tension he was feeling this morning had rubbed off on her.

He shook his head. "I'm on my way out."

He left quickly, before he could make a total fool of himself.

As he let himself into her house a short while later

and inhaled the lemon-and-flower scents that he associated now with Annie, he reminded himself that the month he'd originally granted for this arrangement was over. He'd gotten quite a lot done on her house; he could quit in good conscience now. Of course, it had been kind of nice having his house cleaned regularly, his laundry done, his fridge filled with ready-to-nuke meals. And her house *did* need quite a few more repairs.

Maybe he would give it a couple more weeks. After that, it would probably be better if everything went back to the way it had been before.

"THAT WAS VERY GOOD, Sam," Annie told the six-and-a-half-year-old boy on the piano bench beside her the following Monday afternoon. "You have a lot of natural talent."

The boy seemed pleased. "I like music."

"You still want to learn how to play the piano?"

His head bobbed affirmatively. "I want to play like John Tesh."

His stepmother, Jamie McBride, had entered the room just in time to hear that statement. She laughed and rested a hand on Sam's shoulder. "Sammy's the only six-year-old in his class who would rather listen to John Tesh than the latest pop group. He saw him on TV at Christmas and he's been playing at the piano ever since. We've tried to find a teacher for him, but the few local teachers were either booked up or think he's too young to start."

"Oh, I don't think so." Annie gave the boy a bracing smile. "I think Sam's old enough as long he's willing to do what it takes to learn. And that means practicing at least twenty minutes a day to start out, even longer as you progress further. Do you want to do that, Sam?"

He nodded eagerly. "I'll practice an *hour* a day."

Annie chuckled. "Eventually, you may very well practice that long, and more, but there's no need to burn yourself out at the beginning. Would you like to play for your mom now?"

Jamie raised her eyebrows. "You learned to play something in your first lesson?"

He beamed. "Two songs. One's called 'Happy Hands' and the other is 'Buzzy Bees.' Do you want to hear them?"

"Of course I want to hear them."

His lower lip gripped between his teeth in concentration, Sam positioned his right hand on the keyboard, looking at Annie for confirmation that he was beginning correctly. She nodded encouragingly. The boy drew a deep breath and stared intently at the open music book in front of him as he played the very simple, four-measure melodies Annie had taught him during the past hour.

Jamie applauded enthusiastically when he finished. "Sam, that was great! I can't wait until your dad hears you. Who'd have thought you'd be able to play the piano after your very first lesson?"

He gave her a reality-check look. "It wasn't very hard."

She laughed and ruffled his blond hair. "Give me a break, will you? If you're going to take piano lessons, I reserve the right to be disgustingly proud every time you learn something new."

Though he was smiling, Sam made a production of

rolling his blue eyes. "Oh, man. This is going to be embarrassing."

"Bet on it," Jamie assured him cheerfully.

Annie noticed that the boy didn't look particularly dismayed. Quite the opposite, actually.

She stood and stepped away from the piano bench. "That's the end of our first lesson. Practice your exercises and I'll see you next Monday after school, okay, Sam?"

He nodded, his attention already focused again on the music book in front of him. "See you, Ms. Stewart."

Jamie motioned toward the doorway. "Would you join me in the kitchen for a cup of coffee, Annie?"

"Yes, I'd like that."

Jamie led the way through her comfortably decorated house to the kitchen. She had just filled two good-size mugs with fresh-brewed coffee when they were joined by Abbie, who was almost three.

"Juice?" she asked Jamie hopefully.

Jamie obligingly poured apple juice into a spillproof toddler cup, handed it to the blue-eyed, blond cherub, then joined Annie at the table. "Sam certainly seems to have enjoyed his first piano lesson."

"I can tell he's going to learn quickly. You were right, Jamie. He has a genuine affinity for the piano."

Jamie beamed. "Of course. I know real talent when I see it."

"Yes, I suppose you do." Annie knew from gossip that Jamie had spent nearly ten years working as an actress in New York before moving back to Honoria almost two years ago to teach drama at the high school.

Some people had expressed surprise that the flamboyant redhead had married Trevor McBride, a conservative lawyer and widowed father of two. Having seen Jamie and Trevor together on a couple of occasions at his office, Annie had sensed the deep, loving bond between the couple that had made their differences irrelevant. And it was very obvious that Jamie was crazy about her stepchildren.

"Speaking of talent...have you ever done any acting?" Jamie asked, studying her guest in a manner that almost looked assessing.

A bit warily, Annie asked, "Not since college. Why?"

"I knew it. You were a music major—musical theater?"

"Piano, mostly, but I had a few singing roles. What—"

"Have you ever longed to be back on stage? Missed the sound of applause ringing in your ears?"

Though she couldn't help smiling at Jamie's whimsical questions, Annie still asked, "What are you talking about?"

"I'm involved with the Honoria Community Theater. We've done a couple of plays already, but now everyone wants to put on a musical for the first time. Would you be interested in trying out, maybe for a fall performance?"

Annie didn't know if she would still be in Honoria in the fall. She hadn't planned that far ahead. As for performing in a musical... "I don't know, Jamie. It's been a long time since I've done anything like that. And I'm really not sure I would have the time."

"Think about it, okay? We'd love to have you. We'll be holding auditions in early June."

"I'll think about it," Annie promised, though her first impulse was to refuse on the spot. She'd been fairly content to live in the shadows lately; she wasn't sure she wanted to take a chance at losing that comfortable anonymity.

"So how are things going with the repairs on your house?" Jamie asked, obligingly changing the subject. "Trevor told me he and Trent worked on your roof. Did it help? Is it still leaking?"

Surprised, Annie asked, "Did you say your husband worked on my roof?" It was the first she'd heard of it.

"You didn't know?"

"No." She bit her lower lip.

Now it was Jamie's turn to look surprised. "Does that bother you?"

"A bit."

"Why?"

"I haven't paid him anything. The arrangement I have with his brother is that I clean his house in exchange for the repair work."

"Trevor doesn't want to be paid to help out a friend. And besides, you clean his offices and you're giving Sam piano lessons."

"But he's paying me for both of those. I still come out in his debt."

"So you can do him a favor sometime," Jamie said with a shrug. "Don't worry about it, Annie. It isn't charity."

Jamie had zeroed in on the reason for Annie's discomfort, of course. She'd been so adamant about making her own way, about not needing assistance from anyone, that even the suggestion of charity made her uncomfortable. It was the reason she'd been so anxious to repay Trent for his work and for the rocker he'd given her. She never again wanted to feel as though she was living off someone else.

Jamie didn't let the conversation lag. "How's your arrangement with Trent working out? He's been helpful to you?"

"Extremely," Annie said fervently. "You wouldn't believe how much he's accomplished during the past six weeks."

"He did the cabinets in here, did you know? Trevor and I remodeled a few months ago, and Trent helped us out. He wasn't quite as far along in his recovery then as he is now, but he still managed to do most of it by himself, with Trevor helping only a little. It took a lot of nagging on Trevor's part to get him to do it, though. Trent seemed to be afraid he'd mess it up, though I don't know why since he built all the cabinets in his parents' house when he was home from the Air Force Academy one summer holiday. Working at your place has been good for him, I think," Jamie mused without pausing for breath. "It's getting him out of his house, making him think about someone other than himself. He needed that. He's gotten very self-centered lately."

Annie couldn't help frowning. "He's hardly self-centered. He's worked so hard on my house—much harder than I have at his. I'm sure he's practically exhausted himself, but he just keeps going back. I've never asked him to do anything except fix my front step, but he's done so much more—all on his own."

Jamie's eyebrows rose in response to Annie's spirited defense of Trent. "I wasn't really criticizing him. Just making a comment."

Annie cleared her throat. "It's just that I'm very grateful to him. I couldn't have afforded to pay anyone for all the work he's done for me."

A quick, sharp rap on the back door interrupted the conversation, to Annie's relief. Her relief turned to self-consciousness when Jamie opened the door and the man they had just been discussing walked in.

3

ANNIE WAS AWARE that Trent didn't spot her immediately. Focusing on Jamie, he motioned toward the miniature wooden rocker he had carried in. "I finished Abbie's chair. I made it as tiltproof as possible, but teach her not to stand up in it."

"I will. Oh, Trent, it's perfect. She'll love rocking in it while she watches cartoons." She reached up to kiss his cheek, a gesture he accepted with a resignation that indicated he'd expected a reaction of that sort.

Just the thought of kissing Trent so casually made Annie's mouth go dry. She told herself to quit being an idiot, but that seemed to be an impossible task when Trent McBride was around.

Jamie motioned for him to set the chair on the floor and turned to her little stepdaughter. "Abbie, come look at the chair Uncle Trent made for you. Isn't it beautiful?"

Abbie promptly climbed onto the chair, plopping her bottom on the child-size seat. "Mine," she said, beginning to rock with enthusiasm.

"She loves it." Still smiling, Jamie motioned toward the table. "Annie and I are having coffee, Trent. Would you like to join us?"

Annie saw Trent's startled reaction before he quickly masked it. She was surprised that he hadn't already noticed her sitting there, but apparently he'd been concentrating on his niece. Pushing his glasses up on his nose, he turned to face her, his characteristically somber eyes searching her face in the way that always made her toes curl. *You really are an idiot, Annie.*

He greeted her curtly. "Hello."

It was only further proof of the strange hold he had on her that the sound of his voice affected her so strongly every time she heard it. She couldn't understand it. It was just a voice, after all—a deep, slightly rough-edged growl of a voice, but nothing special. Right?

She offered him an exaggeratedly airy smile. "Hello, Mr. McBride."

Jamie rolled her eyes. "You call him 'Mr. McBride'? Why? You two are the same age, for Pete's sake, and you've known each other for—what?—six weeks? What's with the formality?"

"I never asked her to call me 'mister.'" Trent sounded defensive.

He had never corrected her, either. Annie assumed he liked the professional distance the formality kept between them.

Still sitting in her chair, Abbie held up her cup, offering her uncle a drink. "Juice?"

He looked down at his niece, and his smile softened his stern face in a way that made Annie's silly heart flutter. "I'll have coffee, instead, but thanks, Abbie."

Annie noticed that his voice was several degrees warmer when he talked to the child. There was genuine affection in his expression. As she had suspected all along, Trent wasn't nearly as gruff and curmudgeonly as he liked to pretend.

Looking quite at home, he reached into a cabinet, pulled out a mug and poured himself a cup of coffee. Rather than joining Annie at the table, he leaned back against the counter to sip his drink. He made no effort to initiate conversation, but seemed to be waiting for Annie or Jamie to speak to him. Annie couldn't think of a thing to say. Having Trent's somber eyes on her completely cleared her mind.

Fortunately Sam chose that moment to join them. Carrying his music book, he moved to stand beside Annie, showing no surprise at seeing his uncle. "Hi, Uncle Trent. Ms. Stewart, is it okay if I try to play the next song in the book? This one called 'Sleepy Lion'?"

Since that piece was clearly numbered and very similar to the ones he'd already played, Annie nodded, encouraging his enthusiasm and relieved to have something to distract her from the awkwardness of the situation. "Of course, Sam. Just remember that here and here, you play with your left hand—second finger—and the rest is with your right hand, fingers two, three and four. Okay?"

"Okay. Ms. Stewart gave me a piano lesson, Uncle Trent," Sam said, eager to share his accomplishment. "I already learned two songs. Do you want to hear me play them?"

"Yeah, sure. I'd like to hear them sometime."

"I'll go practice." Sam ran eagerly from the room.

"I hope he'll always be that excited about practicing," Jamie murmured.

Annie chuckled. "I can almost guarantee you that there will come a time when he'll need a bit of prodding—but that's true of nearly every child. I went through a stage when my father had to nag me almost every day to practice, but I'm glad now that he didn't let me quit."

Trent was studying her even more closely now, making it difficult for her not to squirm in her seat. "You give piano lessons?"

She tried to speak lightly. "Sam's my only student at the moment, but I have experience teaching piano."

"Annie has a master's degree in music," Jamie said, moving beside Trent to refill her coffee cup.

Suppressing a wince, Annie wished she hadn't mentioned her degree to Trevor. She hadn't meant to—it had just sort of slipped out when they'd been making conversation as she'd cleaned his offices last week. While chatting about his children, Trevor had told her of Sam's desire to learn to play piano and their futile search for a teacher. The next thing she'd known, Annie had divulged her degree and had mentioned that she'd taught piano while she attended college. She hadn't added that she'd started teaching because she enjoyed working with children in music, not because she'd needed the money.

She had learned today that she could take just as much joy in teaching even though she was being paid for it.

"You have a master's degree in music?" Trent sounded a little skeptical.

She nodded, bracing herself for the question that was sure to follow.

He reacted exactly as she had predicted. "Then how come you're cleaning houses instead of doing something with your education?"

"Trent!" Though notably plainspoken herself, even

Jamie seemed to think her brother-in-law had crossed the line with that blunt question.

Tact was not a word Annie had come to associate with Trent, which probably explained why she wasn't particularly offended. "A music degree isn't the most practical background for earning a living, but there always seems to be a demand for housekeeping services. I don't mind cleaning, and it's a job that lets me feel useful and still independent, so it seemed a logical way to support myself when I moved into the house my great-uncle left me. I like teaching piano, so I'm considering taking on more students, but I'll keep my cleaning business going for now."

"What made you decide to settle in Honoria, Annie?" Jamie seemed as curious as Trent, if considerably more subtle. "Was your great-uncle your only family?"

Since Annie didn't want to talk about her estrangement from her parents, she chose to ignore the second question. "Actually, I needed to make a change in my life and the house my great-uncle left me appeared to be a good place to make a fresh start. When I came to look at it, I was taken with what a pretty and peaceful place Honoria seemed to be—exactly what I needed at the time. Everyone has been very kind to me here, and I'm building up a large clientele for my business, so I've decided to stay for a while."

Jamie smiled. "I know what it's like to start over. I did that when I left New York to come back here to teach. Of course, I had no idea quite how drastically my life would change. I came back single, with very little family, and now I have a husband, two children, nieces, nephews and assorted other in-laws," she added, patting Trent's cheek with a bold familiarity that Annie suspected only Jamie could carry off.

Trent merely gave his sister-in-law a look and set his now-empty cup in the sink. "Thanks for the coffee, Jamie. Tell Sam I'd like him to play for me next time I come by. Annie, I'll see you in the morning."

He glanced at her as he spoke, and their gazes locked for a moment. Annie felt her toes curl inside her sneakers—as they had a tendency to do every time Trent McBride looked at her this way.

"Trevor should be home soon, Trent," Jamie said quickly. "Why don't you stay for dinner?"

Breaking the visual contact with Annie, he shook his head. "Thanks, but I have other plans. See you later."

He left then without looking back.

"But..." Jamie sighed as the door closed behind him. She turned back to Annie, her expression rueful. "I guess he was ready to leave."

Dragging her gaze away from that closed door, Annie nodded, drawing her first full breath since her gaze had been captured by Trent's. "Apparently he was."

"He didn't like us talking about making a new start with our lives, I suppose. That subject's still too raw for Trent. I...um...assume you've heard that his air force career ended with a plane crash a little more than a year and a half ago."

"Yes."

"Of course you have. You've probably figured out by now that Honoria has the most efficient rumor mill in the world."

"Well, yes, I..."

"Trent's having trouble adjusting to the forced changes in his life. All he ever wanted to do was fly, and now that's been taken from him. I didn't know him very well before the crash—Trevor and I had only been dating a short while when it happened, and I hadn't seen Trent since high school—but I understand he was very different before. Trevor said Trent's always been moody, but before the crash he was more extroverted and jovial. He was cocky and self-confident and wisecracking, the life-of-the-party type. I guess that's hard for you to believe."

Annie thought of the emotional pain she'd sensed in Trent the first time she'd met him. She had no problem believing that his accident had changed him. She'd been changed by recent events herself. There'd been a time when she'd been blindly naive, dependent and pathetically eager to please. While she hoped she had avoided the bitterness Trent's accident had left behind, she could identify well enough with his anger and regret. An airplane crash had altered Trent's life; Preston Dixon, with his lies and empty promises, had changed hers.

Because she still didn't feel comfortable talking about Trent behind his back, she changed the subject by glancing at her watch and rising to her feet. "I'd better go," she said. "I have offices to clean."

Jamie stood to escort her out. "I'll see you next week for Sam's lesson, if not before. Do you mind if I give your number to a couple of other parents who are looking for a piano teacher?"

"Not at all. I'll find a way to work their students into my schedule if they're interested." Annie was actually pleased by the prospect of finally putting her education to use, something her father and her former fiancé had mockingly predicted she would never be able to do.

As soon as Trent opened his door for her the following Friday morning, Annie could tell he was in a bad mood. His jaw was hard, his mouth set in a grim line. Though his head was lowered so she couldn't meet his eyes, she thought she saw shadows of pain through the lenses of his glasses. "Are you all right?" she asked impulsively.

His chin lifted. "I'm fine. There are a couple loads of dirty laundry in the hamper. I could use some clean jeans if you have time to wash."

"I'll make time." She watched as he moved toward the door. He was definitely walking stiffly, and she sensed that he was hurting. She also knew he was likely to bite her head off if she expressed concern or in any other way acknowledged that she had noticed his discomfort. Still, she felt the need to try. "You know there's really not much more to do at my house, so if you'd like to take the day off..."

He looked at her then, his expression openly disbelieving. "Not much more to do? Have you actually *looked* at your house lately?"

She knew there was still plenty of work to be done, but she was trying to give him an excuse to rest a day. She should have known his stiff-necked pride would get in the way. "You've done so much for me already," she offered weakly. "I feel as though I'm falling behind in repaying you."

His eyebrows drew even more tightly together, and she almost sighed. She had handled this badly, letting

her concern for him show through her usually carefully maintained professional distance. She knew he
was oversensitive about his disabilities, whatever they
were; she should have known he would not concede
any sort of weakness in front of her. To the contrary,
he was likely to try to do twice as much as usual just to
prove he could.

And what was *really* bothering her was this feeling
that she was beginning to know him so well, despite
the very limited nature of the time they had spent together so far.

"We have an arrangement," he said shortly.
"You've been doing your part, and I intend to uphold
mine."

She caved. "All right. The knob on the medicine
cabinet in my bathroom came off in my hand this
morning. I tried to put it back on, but I think the screw
is stripped."

He nodded. "Anything else?"

"The window in the living room won't open. It was
so warm and pretty yesterday, I wanted to let some
fresh air in, but it was stuck."

"Is that it?"

"If you could just fix those two things today, I'd be
grateful." She figured neither task would demand too
much from him physically—and maybe he would feel
he'd done his part today if he accomplished at least
that much. As she watched him cross the room and
open the door, she wished she could make him understand that he'd already done so much more than she'd
ever expected.

"Mule-headed male," she muttered as the door
closed behind him.

The door opened again. "I heard that," Trent informed her. And then closed the door behind him with a snap.

Annie was startled into a laugh. Had she actually seen a glint of amusement in Trent's usually grim blue eyes? Had that been a wry smile playing around the corners of his hard, straight mouth?

Her laughter fading, she groaned and rubbed her temples. She really didn't want to make Trent smile. He had a strong enough effect on her when he was being rude and irritable.

IT TOOK Trent less than twenty minutes to replace the screw on Annie's old-fashioned wooden medicine-cabinet door and reattach a round ceramic knob. The cabinet needed to be stripped, sanded and repainted, he noted. Actually, the whole place needed painting, inside and out. With spring weather just setting in, it was a good time to get started on that project. He'd have to figure out a way to ask Annie if she wanted to invest in paint.

He found himself chuckling softly as he moved into the living room to check the problem window she'd told him about. He was remembering her disgruntled summation of his character when he'd refused to take the day off. "Mule-headed male," she'd called him.

His amusement faded when he considered why she'd been so determined to talk him out of working today. She'd obviously noticed that he was having one of his bad days—he'd woken up stiff and achy that morning, his back muscles in spasms—but he was still perfectly capable of putting in a couple of hours at her place.

He'd given their service-swapping arrangement a couple more weeks, but every time he thought about ending it, he found himself making excuses to prolong it. He'd tried to convince himself that he'd grown spoiled to having his house cleaned and his laundry done. He'd thought of all the repairs still waiting to be done on Annie's house, and he'd told himself he was being noble and generous to help her out.

But the truth was, he thought as he studied the sticking window casing, he had needed this more than Annie did. From his initial evaluation of her house to the prioritizing and implementing of repairs, he had secretly relished the sense of purpose he'd found since he'd begun this project. For two mornings a week, he'd had a reason to get out of bed. Something to do besides sit alone in his house and brood about the loss of his dreams. Dreams he had shattered himself through his own recklessness.

Scowling, he gripped the window handles in both hands and jerked upward. Pain body-slammed him from behind, making him stagger and then go down to his knees. Breaking into a sick sweat, he tried to stand—only to be brought down again.

Maybe he would just stay right where he was for a little while, he thought grimly, lowering himself carefully to the floor and letting the waves of pain wash over him.

ANNIE USUALLY CLEANED another house on Friday after leaving Trent's place, but because her client had canceled that day, she found herself with several free hours. She made a stop by Honoria's only music store, placed an order for some piano-teaching supplies, then headed home for what she anticipated would be a rare few hours of leisure.

She assumed Trent would have already finished for the day. She certainly hadn't expected to find him lying facedown on her living-room floor.

"Trent?" She knelt beside him, her heart in her throat. His eyes were closed, his glasses lying on the floor beside him. A sheen of perspiration covered his face, even though the room was cool.

She was relieved when his eyes opened, though the expression in them almost made her gulp. Trent was *not* happy to have been found this way by her. "What's wrong?" she asked.

"Muscle spasms in my back. It's no big deal. It happens sometimes." His attempt at nonchalance didn't exactly come off since the sentence ended in a gasp.

"How long have you been lying here?"

"Half an hour, maybe."

"I'll call an ambulance."

"No. My cell phone's in my pocket. If I'd wanted an ambulance, I'd have called one."

"Can you stand up?"

"Of course I can stand." He made an effort to rise, paled, and lowered himself carefully back down. "Just not right now."

"All right, that's it—I'm calling for help."

"No!" He reached out to grab her wrist when she would have risen. For a man who couldn't even stand, his grip was remarkably strong. "Don't call anyone."

"Trent, you need help. Just let me—"

"No." He swallowed, then added. "Please."

Apparently he'd swallowed a large amount of pride. Annie groaned, annoyed with herself for letting his plea affect her. "What am I supposed to do? Pretend you aren't here? Just go about my business and step over you when I want to get to the other side of the room? Toss a throw rug over you, perhaps?"

His eyebrows dipped lower. "I never realized until today that you have such a smart mouth on you," he grumbled.

"Yeah, well, you would try the patience of a saint. So what are we going to do, Trent?"

"I gave in and took a muscle relaxer a few minutes ago. When it kicks in, I'll be able to get up and go home."

"If it's like any muscle relaxer I've ever taken, you won't be able to drive when it takes effect. You're already starting to float, aren't you?"

He made a visible effort to focus on her face. She didn't know how well he could see without his glasses, but she suspected the glazed look in his eyes had more to do with medication than myopia. "I can handle it," he muttered.

She shook her head. "Do you *ever* ask for help, Trent McBride?"

"Do *you*?" he countered.

He had her there. "At least let me call your brother."

He shook his head. "He'll tell Mom, and she'll freak out and start hovering. She and Dad are planning to leave for a month-long cruise in a few weeks, and I don't want to give her reason to delay it again. They both need the vacation very badly after everything that's happened in our family during the past couple of years."

She didn't know what had happened in his family,

but it was an argument she couldn't really refute. His concern for his parents obviously outweighed his own discomfort, and she wouldn't have felt right going against his wishes. Painfully estranged from her own parents, she could only envy the close bonds she'd sensed in the McBride family. She could also identify with Trent's need to prove himself independent of them.

"What do you want me to do?" she asked more gently. "Would a heating pad help?"

"Yeah." He didn't express his gratitude that she'd given up her insistence to call for help, but she saw it in his expression. "Thanks."

"If I help you, can you make it to the couch?"

"I think so," he answered cautiously.

"I'll get the heating pad first. Don't try to move—I'll be right back."

"I'm not going anywhere," he muttered.

She hurried into the bedroom, still half convinced she should be calling an ambulance instead of trying to take care of him herself.

She should have known that Trent wouldn't follow directions even when he was in terrible pain. She found him struggling to rise when she returned with the heating pad in hand. Making a sound of exasperation, she tossed the pad on the couch and moved to help him.

"You really *are* mule-headed, aren't you?" she chided, bracing him with her shoulder. Her reaction to seeing his pallor and the pain in his eyes made her voice sharper than she had intended. "I told you to wait until I got back."

"If I wanted to be lectured, I'd have called my

mother," he complained, his words slurred because he was forcing them through clenched teeth.

"Something we should probably be doing, anyway," she retorted, all too aware of his body pressed full-length against hers. She had one arm around his waist, which confirmed her belief that he could stand to gain a few pounds. She could feel heat radiating through his washed-thin denim shirt. She pushed her instinctive feminine reactions to the back of her mind and concentrated on his welfare.

Lowering him to the couch was an ordeal in itself. She blinked back a film of sympathetic tears when a broken gasp escaped him. He was hurting so badly and she felt so helpless.

He barely fit on her secondhand couch. She slipped a throw pillow beneath his head and managed to position the heating pad at the small of his back, where he said the pain was most intense. She retrieved his glasses from the floor and set them on the coffee table within easy reach. "Can I get you anything?" she asked then, hovering beside the couch. "Something to drink? Soda? Hot tea, perhaps?"

"No, I'm okay for now. If you have houses to clean or something, feel free to go. I'll just lie here a few minutes until the medication does its job, then I'll head home."

As anxious as he seemed to be for her to leave him to suffer in solitude, Annie had no intention of doing so. Nor did she intend to allow him to drive home. She wasn't sure how she was going to accomplish that, exactly—whether it would involve calling his brother or simply threatening to do so—but she couldn't stand back and let him do anything that foolish.

She would, however, refrain from hovering over him. "I have some things to do in the kitchen," she told him. "Call out if you need me."

He nodded, avoiding her eyes. "I'll be fine."

He wasn't fine, of course. He looked miserable. Hurting, embarrassed, chagrined. As much as she hated leaving him, she knew he wanted privacy. Just to give herself something productive to do, she went into the kitchen and began to make lasagna, her hands busy but her thoughts focused on the man in the other room.

Everything she had heard about Trent McBride during the past couple of months reinforced her belief that he must hate being in this awkward situation. He'd apparently been accustomed to being treated like a local hero. Star athlete in school, extremely popular with the local girls, then on to the Air Force Academy, where he had excelled in his studies. She could imagine how dashing he must have looked in his pilot's uniform.

It had to be galling for a man like that to be found on the floor, unable to walk even a few steps on his own.

She made herself wait twenty minutes before checking on him. He was asleep when she tiptoed into the living room. The pain medication he had taken must be strong, she thought, studying the hollows beneath his eyes. She wondered if he always carried it with him or if it had been a lucky coincidence that he'd had it today.

Funny how young he looked when he slept, she mused, unable to resist lingering another moment. She'd gotten into the habit of thinking of him as older than herself, when they were actually the same age.

She realized now that the shallow lines around his eyes and mouth had been etched there by chronic pain. And even though she knew he would hate it, her heart twisted in sympathy.

He stirred restlessly against the throw pillow and she moved swiftly toward the door. She didn't want him to wake up and find her watching him sleep. But as she returned to the kitchen, it occurred to her that she wouldn't have minded standing there watching him a while longer.

4

TRENT WOKE disoriented, groggy and still uncomfortable enough that he concentrated first on the pain, then on his surroundings. He grimaced when he realized where he was and remembered how he'd gotten there.

It humiliated him that Annie had found him sprawled on her floor, utterly incapacitated. After his arrogant assurances to her that morning, his unreliable back had chosen the worst possible time to fail him. Now he had to face her again, see the pity in her eyes, resign himself to having Annie—like everyone else—treat him as an invalid from here on.

Which only went to show how foolish he'd been to start imagining that Annie needed his help. He'd rather liked believing he had something worthwhile to offer her, even if only physical labor. Lately he'd even found himself wondering if maybe he should ask her out sometime, just to see if she might be interested in something besides his skill with power tools. Not that he'd been thinking long term, or anything, he assured himself quickly. He just thought maybe they could keep each other company occasionally. But that seemed unlikely, now that she'd seen him at his worst. Even if she agreed, he wouldn't know if she'd accepted his invitation because she liked him, or because she felt sorry for him—something he simply wouldn't tolerate.

Their arrangement had been pretty good while it had lasted, he thought glumly, but it was over now. She wouldn't want him doing any more repairs for fear that he might hurt himself, and he would be damned if he let her work for him without accepting his help in return.

Moving very carefully, he slid his legs off the side of the couch and pushed himself upright. His back muscles clenched in protest, but he ignored them, rising slowly but relatively steadily to his feet. Sliding his glasses onto his nose, he remembered that Annie had said she would be in the kitchen. The tantalizing aromas coming from that direction let him know she'd been busy. Bracing himself for cloying sympathy, he made his way stiffly toward the kitchen.

Annie was sitting at the table, a glass of iced tea beside her, an open paperback in her hands. She looked up when he entered. Her eyes widened, then narrowed assessingly. "You look a little better," she said, her voice surprisingly matter-of-fact.

"Yeah. Better." Marginally, but he would take what he could get.

"Are you hungry? It's almost two o'clock and I don't suppose you've eaten since breakfast."

He hadn't eaten breakfast, actually. Just coffee. He was surprised to realize that he was hungry.

"I made lasagna," she said when he hesitated. "I was just about to have some, myself. Why don't you join me?"

Lasagna just happened to be one of his favorite foods. He might as well join her for lunch since she was offering and he saw no evidence of the pity he had dreaded. He'd consider it a farewell meal, of sorts. "Sounds good. Thanks."

She set her book aside and motioned him toward the rickety-looking wooden chair across the table— the only other seat available in the small kitchen. "What would you like to drink? I have tea, cola, juice..."

He chose the tea, then sank slowly into the chair. It rocked a little when he sat in it. Some wood glue and putty would reinforce it, he thought automatically. Next time he was here, he would...

He brought himself up short, reminding himself there probably wouldn't be a next time.

Annie set a well-filled plate of lasagna and steamed vegetables in front of him, along with a glass of iced tea. "Is there anything else I can get for you?"

"No, this is fine. Um...do you always eat this well for lunch?"

She chuckled as she settled across the table with her own plate. "Hardly. I usually just have a sandwich or a liquid-meal replacement. But I had a couple of cancellations today, so I'm free until five, which is when I clean your father and brother's offices."

"So you made lasagna."

Her smile turned wry. "It gave me something to do besides hover over you and worry."

Taking a bite, he silently approved her choice. "There was no reason for you to worry about me."

"Of course. What was I thinking? I come home all the time to find men lying on my floor grimacing in pain. I realize now I shouldn't have given it even a second thought."

He wondered why he'd once thought of Annie as a meek little doormat. Apparently she had made it a point to hide the fact that there was an acerbic sense of irony hidden behind her delicate fragility. Since he couldn't think of an appropriate response, he took another bite of the delicious lasagna to avoid having to answer.

They ate a few minutes in silence and then Annie spoke again. "I assume you injured your back in the plane crash?"

He nodded, not surprised that she'd heard about the accident.

"Are you being treated for it?"

He lifted one shoulder in a slight shrug. "I've had a couple of operations, but there's not much more that can be done."

"What about therapy? Exercises?"

Focusing fiercely on his plate, he muttered, "I've been given some exercises, but they don't help much."

"Why do I suspect you don't do them as faithfully as you should?"

Now she sounded like his mother. He gave her a look, then reached for his tea.

Propping her chin on one hand, she studied him openly, making him self-conscious. "What?" he asked.

"I was just remembering the first time I met you. I'd heard the whispers around town and I wasn't sure what to expect."

He scowled. "I hope you've learned that you can't believe everything you hear in this town. People around here have made a sport out of gossiping about the McBrides. It's been going on since my great-grandfather's day."

"So I've been told. One of my clients is Martha Godwin."

His scowl deepened. "She's the worst of the bunch. What did she tell you about me?"

"Only that you were in a terrible accident that left you with serious injuries. She probably would have embellished, but I don't encourage gossip about my clients."

"Good policy," he muttered, stabbing his fork into a tender baby carrot.

"From what little she did say about you, I half expected to find you in a wheelchair. Missing a few limbs at the least."

"I sat in a wheelchair for almost four months after the crash. I didn't care for it."

She chuckled. "I don't imagine that you did."

He still hated the thought of her picturing him as an invalid—even though he had to admit she wasn't treating him like one. "I've been on my feet for months. I've been left with a trick back and limited peripheral vision, but I get by just fine."

She glanced at his glasses. "So that's why you didn't see me sitting at Jamie's table the other day. I wondered."

He pushed his near-empty plate away as he remembered his surprise at finding her in his sister-in-law's kitchen. Knowing she had been watching him while he was unaware of her presence had made him extremely uncomfortable. Now she knew everything about him, he thought in resignation. Now would come the pity.

"You were lucky, weren't you?" she startled him by asking instead.

He stared at her in disbelief. *"Lucky?"* That was one word he hadn't associated with himself since the accident.

Her eyebrows rose. "Of course. You survived an airplane crash. You're still in one piece, you're able to do beautiful woodworking and you have a wonderful, loving family. You're still prettier than any man has a right to be. All in all, I would say you're very lucky."

Who *was* this woman? he asked himself, dismayed to feel his cheeks warm in response to being called "pretty." His meek, shy little housekeeper had turned into someone he didn't know at all.

"Now," she continued, pushing her plate away, "do you want to stay here and rest for another couple of hours or do you want me to take you home?"

"I'm perfectly capable of driving myself home."

"I would be willing to bet the medication you took has a warning not to drive or operate heavy machinery after taking it."

He shrugged. He was still floating a little, but he felt capable of driving the short distance home. At least the spasms in his back had dulled to a steady ache rather than the stabbing pains from earlier. "I'll be fine."

"Don't be silly, Trent. You can hardly move and you're high on pills. What kind of friend would I be if I let you drive in this condition?"

He hadn't realized she considered herself a friend of any kind. As far as he knew, they were merely acquaintances. At least, that was what he'd been trying to convince himself of during the past few weeks, even though he was aware that he'd spent entirely too much of that time thinking about her. Wondering about her. Picturing her pretty face and slender body in his mind. And he definitely liked the sound of his name on her lips.

"How would your cousin, the police chief, feel about you driving under the influence?" she added.

"Wade isn't my cousin. He's married to my cousin Emily."

"Would the family connection keep him from giving you a ticket if you get pulled over?"

"No," he admitted dryly. "He'd be more likely to handcuff me. But I won't be pulled over. I'm okay to drive."

She frowned at him. "I can't force you to stay, of course, or to let me take you home. But if you're determined to drive, I'll follow you, just to make sure you get there safely."

"That isn't..."

"Trent—just stop arguing, will you? You're giving me a headache."

A snort of laughter escaped him before he could stop it. "Damn," he muttered, amused despite himself. "You sound like my mother."

She smiled at him. "I should probably take that as a compliment. Your mother seems like a very capable and well-respected woman."

"My mother is terrifying," he said, surreptitiously rubbing his lower back beneath the table.

Annie glanced at her watch. "I don't have to leave for another two hours or so. By that time, your medication should have worn off and you'll be safe to drive as long as you're feeling better. Why don't you hang out here and take it easy until then?"

"I don't want to be in your way," he said stiffly.

"You won't be. I was planning to use this afternoon to be totally lazy. It's my first day off in a while, and I'm going to spend it finding out who the murderer is in this book. You can stretch out on the couch, rest your back and watch TV or read or something, if you like. That's what you'd do if you were home, isn't it? At least until you feel better. You don't want to do anything to set off the spasms again."

No, he didn't want that. He was just now able to breathe deeply again, and the thought of climbing into his truck and driving over the bumpy gravel road that led to his secluded cottage wasn't particularly appealing just then. If Annie's manner had been at all patronizing or coddling, he'd have left in a minute. But her brusque, rather challenging attitude was exactly what he needed to put him at ease.

"So you like mysteries?" he asked, nodding toward the book she'd been reading when he'd joined her.

"I read everything. I'm sure we can find something for you."

"Then I guess I'll hang around for a while. But only until the medicine wears off."

"Can you make it to the living room okay?"

"Of course I can make it." To prove his point, he rose too quickly and had to grip the table to steady himself. "Eventually," he added ruefully.

She'd made an instinctive move toward him when he faltered, but she settled back and spoke in a tone he suspected was deliberately casual. "Make yourself comfortable in there. You'll find my books on the case on the back wall—I'm sure you know where everything is by now. I'll just clear away these dishes and then I'll join you. Can I bring you anything when I come? A cup of coffee, maybe?"

"Sounds good, but don't go to any trouble."

"I was going to make a pot for myself, anyway." She sounded sincere, even though he suspected she wasn't being entirely truthful.

He moved slowly into the other room, selected a mystery from her collection and settled carefully into the rocking chair he had given her. And then he just sat there, thinking about Annie and wondering how she'd managed to talk him into staying.

Maybe she didn't feel particularly sorry for him, after all, he mused. Her matter-of-factness had been just what he had needed to get him past the embarrassment of hurting himself in her house. Maybe their arrangement didn't have to end just yet, after all.

He was definitely surprised to feel himself smiling a little as he opened the book he'd selected. An hour earlier, he hadn't expected to find anything to smile about this afternoon.

ANNIE KNEW that her behavior had effectively ruined the professional relationship she and Trent had developed during their six-week association. She could hardly go back to meekly calling him "Mr. McBride" now and pretending she saw him as just another client. But finding him on her floor earlier had changed everything. She'd realized then how vulnerable his pain made him—and how fragile his ego was since the accident. He'd been visibly surprised to hear her call

him lucky, because he'd gotten out of the habit of
thinking of himself that way.

She'd sensed that he'd dreaded her reaction to finding him incapacitated, and she had understood that
pity was the last thing he wanted. He needed her to be
blunt and matter-of-fact, and she had been—even to
the point of rudeness. He had responded to that much
more favorably than he would have to expressions of
sympathy or concern. But she doubted that they
would ever be able to return to the coolly polite distance they had maintained before.

She dawdled a while cleaning the kitchen, but could
find nothing more to do. Tucking her novel under one
arm, she carried a cup of coffee in each hand when she
joined him in the living room. He was sitting in the
rocker he'd made, and she could see now that the
chair had been built to his personal specifications. The
curved wooden seat and wide-slatted back that she
found so comfortable provided firm support for his
back. His elbows rested easily on the broad arms of
the rocker as he gazed down at the paperback he'd
chosen from her library.

He really was a talented woodworker, she thought,
remembering the beautiful furniture and cabinetry in
his house. She wondered if he had any plans to do it
professionally. As long as he made some common-
sense allowances for his bad back, there was no reason
he shouldn't earn a living doing something he excelled at, was there?

He looked up and she made herself speak casually.
"I brought coffee."

He reached out to accept his cup from her.
"Thanks."

"How's your back?"

"Better."

She settled on the couch with her coffee, laying her book beside her. "Is there anything I can get for you? I have some cookies in the pantry."

"No, I'm fine."

She picked up her book, then sat with it unopened in her lap, her gaze on Trent as he sipped his coffee and turned a page in the paperback. The afternoon sun slanted through the window behind him, turning his hair to gold. Such nice hair, she thought wistfully. She wondered if it felt as soft and springy as it looked.

As if he'd sensed her looking at him, he glanced up. "What?"

She shrugged, embarrassed at being caught staring and relieved he couldn't read her mind. "Nothing. Sorry."

He turned his attention back to the book, took another sip of coffee, then looked up at her again. "If you're waiting for me to do something interesting, I'm afraid this is it."

Her cheeks warmed. "I'm sorry. I keep staring, don't I? I suppose it's because I don't have guests very often. Actually, you're the first."

He closed his book. He didn't seem annoyed when he leaned back in the rocker and held the coffee cup loosely in front of him. "Your first guest, hmm? This probably isn't the way you expected it to be."

"Well, I'd prefer my guests to be here from choice rather than being physically incapable of leaving," she admitted with a smile.

She'd half expected him to frown again at her mention of his earlier predicament, and it caught her a bit off guard when he chuckled, instead.

She didn't know why, but he suddenly seemed to be in an almost mellow mood—mellow for Trent, anyway. Was it the medication? The food? The fact that he was feeling better? Whatever the reason, she decided to enjoy it while it lasted.

She smiled back at him. "All in all, I don't think you're a bad first guest. You stay out of my way, you don't complain—much—and you like my cooking. Or at least you seemed to."

He grimaced. "I'm really a lousy guest, aren't I? I didn't even tell you how good the meal was."

The words pleased her more than they should have. "I'm glad you liked it."

"I already knew you were a good cook. You've been bringing me casseroles ever since I gave you this chair."

"It was the least I could do. I really love the rocker."

He lifted the coffee cup to his lips again. She couldn't help following the movement with her eyes. He had a great mouth, she mused. And when it curved into one of his rare, sexy smiles...

She brought that line of thought to an abrupt end. "I noticed that you fixed the knob on the medicine cabinet."

"Yeah. It just needed a new screw. The, uh, window's still stuck, though."

Apparently, he'd been working on the window when he'd thrown his back out. "That's okay. Maybe you can get to it next time."

He lowered the cup slowly. "Next time?"

Something in his tone puzzled her. "Um, yeah—

next Tuesday? You think you'll be feeling better by then?"

"Undoubtedly. I just wasn't sure you..."

His words faded, leaving her bewildered. Had today's mishap unnerved him so badly that he wasn't sure he wanted to continue the repair work? She could certainly understand if he didn't think he was physically able to continue, but she would be surprised if he admitted it. "You do want me to clean for you next week, don't you?"

"Yeah, sure. If you want to keep it going, of course."

"Well, yes. I mean, if you do. If you're ready to stop, that's okay. You've done so much already and there's not..."

"Actually, your place needs painting. Inside and out, really. It means you'll have to buy paint, of course, but I can get you a discount at the hardware store. And having me do the painting will save you the cost of labor."

"I've been thinking that a fresh coat of paint would brighten things up around here. I considered tackling the job, myself, but I've never painted before and I wasn't sure how to start. I can afford the supplies now, but are you sure painting isn't too...um...?"

"Yes?" His voice was suddenly very soft.

She swallowed, deciding not to mention her concern that painting the house would be too physically demanding for him. She assumed he knew what he could handle. "You're sure it won't be too expensive?" she amended quickly.

She could almost see him relax. "It shouldn't be too bad. We can do a room at a time inside, though the outside will have to be done all at once."

She nodded. "I'll start picking colors."

"You might want to try something different than the gray your great-uncle painted everywhere."

She smiled wryly. "I'm not sure it was originally gray. I think it's all just turned that color with the passage of time."

"You could be right."

"If you're going to start that project here soon, I think I'll do some spring-cleaning at your place, if that's okay with you."

"Like what?"

"Oh, you know—cleaning the pantry, new shelf paper. I could take down the curtains and clean them, and if I rent a carpet shampooer, I could do the rugs."

"You're sure that's not too much for you to take on?" He asked the question with a perfectly straight face, though she knew he was mocking her a bit.

"I think I can handle it," she answered firmly.

He shrugged. "Whatever the place needs."

She finished her coffee, thinking that it was good to know their professional relationship was staying the same, even if she suspected that other things between them had changed.

Trent glanced at his watch. "I know you have other things to do today. I'm going home. And before you start nagging again, the food and coffee have cleared my head. I'm okay to drive."

"You're sure?"

"Positive. Thanks again for the assistance and the meal. And, uh, I'd appreciate it if you didn't mention what happened to anyone."

"I won't. But if it happens again, I hope you'll tell your doctor."

The quelling look he gave her made her bite her lip before she offered any further unsolicited advice.

She walked him to the door, watching for any sign that he shouldn't be doing this. His posture was perhaps rather straighter than usual, his steps measured, but he appeared to be clearheaded and in control. There really seemed to be no reason to delay him any further.

"Satisfied?" he asked at the door, slanting her a look that let her know he'd been aware of her watching him.

She opened the door for him. "I'm sure you'll be fine. But call me if you need anything, okay? You can count on me not to hover."

"I'll see you Tuesday," he said, making it clear he didn't expect to be calling her before then.

She closed the door behind him, then had to fight herself not to peek through the curtains to make sure he made it safely to his truck. He was perfectly capable, she assured herself, and even if he did have a little trouble, he wouldn't want her watching him. Trent's pride had taken enough of a beating in front of her today.

She wondered what it would do for his ego to learn that her feelings for him hadn't changed in the least this afternoon. She still found him the most attractive, most intriguing man she had ever met. The type of man who could make a woman do something incredibly foolish—like fall head over heels for him—if she wasn't very careful.

That frightening thought made her sink into the rocker. She had come to Honoria to be independent, she reminded herself. On her own. She'd broken an engagement to a man who had wanted to own her, manipulate her, control her—the way her father always had—and she didn't trust her own judgment when it came to men just now.

She could still remember the ugly fight she'd had with her father when she'd announced to him on the afternoon of her birthday that she had broken off her engagement to Preston. She had known her father favored the engagement, but she hadn't realized until then just how much he'd been counting on it. Preston, he had informed her, was the son he had always wanted. Whereas she—well, he'd made it pretty clear that the years she'd spent trying to please him, trying to be everything he wanted her to be, had been wasted. He had told her she was passably pretty, but that she would never be able to make it on her own. She was accustomed to money, to physical comfort, to having others take care of her. Just how did she plan to support herself with the frivolous music degree he had paid for?

"I'll scrub floors, if I have to," she had answered flatly. "At least I'll be making my own choices. I'm tired of being your puppet. Nothing I've done has ever pleased you, and I'll be damned if I spend the rest of my life with a man I don't love just to give you the son you wish I had been!"

The rebellion had been building inside her for a long time—years, really. She'd tried more than once to break away, but had always allowed herself to be brought back around, either by her mother's tears or her father's threats. But this time she hadn't let either of them change her mind.

She had needed to prove to herself that she could get by on her own. Which meant she didn't need to be getting involved with anyone for a while yet—especially a difficult man like Trent McBride.

5

THAT AFTERNOON with Trent was the last day of leisure Annie had for the next two weeks. She threw herself into her work with a vengeance, as much to distract herself from her worries about the future as for the money she needed. She took on three new piano students and two more cleaning clients, working some days from seven in the morning until eight in the evening. She didn't mind cleaning—except for a woman named April Penny who never acted quite satisfied with anything Annie did and who seemed annoyed that Annie wouldn't discuss the personal business of her other clients. But it was the piano lessons she particularly enjoyed.

Unfortunately, she couldn't make a living giving lessons to only four students.

There were times when she lay in bed, tired and aching, and asked why she was doing this. She didn't have to work this hard, she reminded herself somberly. She had other options—but all of them involved admitting to herself, if not to her parents, that she couldn't make it on her own. And that was something she had vowed never to do.

Though she had expected awkwardness from Trent the first time they saw each other after the episode at her house, there was no noticeable change. He'd greeted her politely, replied rather testily that he was fine when she asked about his back, then left for her house without further conversation. When she got home that evening, she found a note telling her that her living-room window had been fixed, and her kitchen chairs glued and stabilized. Whatever it had cost him physically, Trent must have been determined to prove himself capable of keeping up his end of the bargain.

She could hardly fault him for that, since she knew just how it felt to need to prove something.

She was surprised to find Trent in his father's office late Friday afternoon two weeks after he'd hurt himself at her house. She was running later than usual and everyone else was gone. Trent was the last person she'd expected to encounter there. "What are you doing?" she asked curiously, watching him stretch a measuring tape across the built-in credenza behind Caleb's desk.

"Dad and Trevor are remodeling the offices. They want new carpet, furnishings and cabinetry. Trevor's decided he wants me to do the cabinets."

"Your brother obviously wanted the best."

To her surprise, Trent looked a little flustered by her compliment. "I tried to convince him to hire a professional, but he seems to think no one else can give him what he wants. This is just a hobby for me, but Trevor acts like I'm some sort of expert."

"Trevor has faith in you because he's seen what you can do—as I have," Annie said, touched by this glimpse of insecurity. "I'm sure the McBride Law Firm will have the most beautiful cabinets in town."

He grunted, the way men do when they're embarrassed. And he looked so cute with a slight flush on his cheeks that Annie had to suppress a totally inappropriate urge to pinch his cheek. She couldn't help wondering what he would do if she gave in to the impish impulse.

"Don't let me keep you from your work," he muttered, pointedly writing numbers on a notepad he'd pulled from the back pocket of his jeans.

She reached for the overflowing wastebasket beneath Caleb's desk. "I won't."

For the next forty-five minutes she went about her business without further conversation with Trent. Which didn't mean, of course, that she was unaware of him. She knew when he completed the measurements in Caleb's office and moved to Trevor's. She heard him moving around in the bathrooms and the reception area, and she made sure to stay out of his way. They performed a rather elaborate dance to make sure they worked in separate rooms, but Annie knew she would never get anything accomplished if Trent was too close by.

She ran out of energy while dusting Trevor's office. Overwhelmed for a moment by a wave of weariness, she sank onto his sofa and leaned her head back. She would have liked to spend the rest of the evening sitting in her rocker with a book and a cup of tea, but that wasn't possible. It had been a long day and it still wasn't over. She needed a few minutes to recharge before she continued. She closed her eyes, took several deep, cleansing breaths and pictured a quiet beach in her mind.

"Are you okay?"

Trent's deep voice brought Annie's eyes open in a

hurry. She hadn't even heard him enter the room. "I'm fine," she assured him, jumping to her feet. "Just resting."

He caught her arm when she would have bustled past him. "Annie?"

She'd worn a short-sleeve T-shirt with her jeans, so his palm was pressed against bare skin. She felt his warmth, the roughness of calluses, the strength of his long fingers. His head was bent toward her, making her vividly aware of the difference between her five feet three inches and his six-foot height.

The last time she'd stood this close to him, he'd been too distracted by pain even to notice her, and she'd been so concerned about him that she'd hardly been aware of his proximity. At least, she'd tried not to notice. But he was hardly incapacitated this time. In fact, he looked strong and solid and heart-stoppingly virile. She swallowed. "What?"

He searched her face. "You look tired."

She wrinkled her nose, trying to hide her self-consciousness behind a quip. "Just what every woman wants to hear. Thanks."

His mouth twisted in a half smile. "The fact that you look tired doesn't make you any less attractive. How many houses did you clean today?"

"Um—three," she murmured, bemusedly wondering if he had just actually said he found her attractive.

He shook his head. "Three in one day is too many, especially when you work here in the evenings. Did you take time for lunch?"

"I had some errands to run at lunchtime. I drank a liquid-meal replacement."

His frown deepened. "At least tell me you're finished for the day."

"I have a piano lesson at seven, but I'm through after that."

"And tomorrow? What's your schedule then?"

"On Saturdays, I clean a real estate office and an accounting firm. And I'm giving another piano lesson tomorrow afternoon. Why are you suddenly so interested in my schedule?"

"Because I can tell you're trying to do too much. Jamie told me you're getting swamped with calls for cleaning and piano lessons. I hope you realize you have to say no sometimes. You can always keep a waiting list if you get more requests than you can handle comfortably."

"I appreciate your concern, Trent, but I'm quite capable of arranging my own schedule."

He didn't look convinced. "Then why do you look so exhausted?"

"You just caught me resting for a minute. I'm fine, Trent. Really."

"But..."

She leveled him a look. "Do you want *me* to start asking about whether you're trying to do too much at my place?"

"Uh—no."

"Then back off, McBride."

He broke into a full grin—and the sheer beauty of it took her breath away. "You really like to think you're tough, don't you?"

She had to clear her throat before she could speak. She hoped her voice sounded relatively normal. "I'm tougher than I look."

He reached up with his free hand to brush a strand of hair away from her cheek. "You'd have to be. You look like a strong wind would blow you over."

Something deep inside her quivered in response to his touch. Her voice was definitely huskier this time. "I'd, uh, better get moving."

"Yeah." But he didn't release her arm.

She looked up inquiringly, her gaze sliding over his face and pausing on his mouth. "Trent?"

He seemed to be looking at her mouth, too. "Mmm?"

"You're still holding my arm."

He was standing so close his breath ruffled her hair. "I know."

"So are you going to..." Her voice faded as her attention locked on the slight indention in his lower lip.

His fingers flexed against her arm, sliding against her skin. "Am I going to what?"

Annie felt her throat contract. Was she imagining things, or was he suddenly looking at her as if the attraction she'd felt for him from the beginning wasn't all one-sided? "Trent, I—"

As if something had suddenly galvanized him into action, he abruptly released her arm and stepped back. "Are you finished here?" he asked, his tone gruff.

She blinked. "I—yes, I think so."

"Come on, I'll walk you out."

She looked around to make sure she hadn't lost anything. Her mind, for instance. "Okay, I'm ready."

She carried the plastic tote and Trent followed with her vacuum cleaner. They loaded them into her car and Trent closed the trunk. "The days are getting longer," he commented, glancing at the cloudless sky.

She nodded, wondering if this was an attempt at making small talk—something he'd rarely bothered with before. When things get too intense, talk about the weather, she'd always heard. "It's getting warmer, too," she said a bit too brightly. "It will be summer soon."

"You know how hot summers can get around here?"

Perhaps this was his way of finding out more about her without actually asking personal questions. "I grew up in Atlanta. I'm well familiar with summers in this area."

He glanced at his watch. "You said you have a piano lesson at seven?"

"Yes."

"That doesn't give you much time for dinner. Want to stop by Cora's with me for a quick sandwich?"

Startled, she hesitated a moment before answering. Was he asking her out—or was this just a friendly gesture to repay her for the meals she had prepared for him? When she spoke, it was a lame, "Uh—you mean now?" *Oh, great, Annie. Real intelligent comment.*

"Yes, now. You've got about forty-five minutes and Cora's is close by. You must be hungry—I know I am."

She had planned to get a drive-through burger and eat in her car, which was undoubtedly the wisest course to take. Yet Trent's offer sounded so much more interesting. She accepted before she had a chance to change her mind. "Okay, but I'll have to hurry."

"Then let's go. I'll follow you."

She climbed into her car, wondering as she started the engine if she really had lost her mind.

"WELL, HEY, Trent. Aren't you a sight for sore eyes?"

Resisting an impulse to wince in response to the loud greeting, Trent merely nodded, instead, to the wide-hipped, frizzy-haired waitress who welcomed them to Cora's Café. "Hey, Mindy. How have you been?"

"Same as always," forty-something Mindy Hooper replied cheerfully. "Still pushing food for grouchy ol' Cora. Been working here more than twenty years, and Cora still has trouble remembering my name." Her hearty laugh indicated that she was only joking.

Aware that many of the diners in the always-crowded, long-established café were watching them with interest, Trent was reminded of why he hadn't gone out in public much since his accident. Everyone always seemed to be staring at him, speculating about him, waiting for him to give them a clue to his thoughts or feelings. They wanted to know about the accident. About his current physical condition. About his plans for the future. They wanted to know what had happened to the Trent McBride they used to know. He had no answers for them.

If he hadn't been so determined to make sure Annie took time to eat, he wouldn't have subjected himself to this attention. It wasn't a date, he assured himself. He just hadn't liked the tired and drawn way she had looked when he'd caught her resting in Trevor's office.

"We've only got a half hour or so, Mindy," he said,

focusing on her instead of the other patrons. "Have you got some sandwiches made up or something?"

"I can do better than that. You two go sit down and I'll have a couple of blue plate specials out in no time."

"We appreciate it." He motioned Annie toward one of the few empty tables, ignoring everyone else as he followed her across the room.

"What do you suppose is on the blue plate special?" she asked, sinking into her chair.

"Whatever it is, it will be hot and filling—just what you need."

She laughed softly. "Now *you* sound like your mother."

"Low blow, Annie."

"I think it's sweet that you're suddenly concerned about whether I'm eating enough."

He grimaced. She was calling him sweet again—even though he knew she was teasing him. He was going to have to try harder to resist these impulses to be nice to her before she formed an entirely wrong idea about his character. "I just want you to stay healthy so you can keep cleaning my house," he muttered.

Annie just laughed.

True to her promise, Mindy appeared then with heaping plates of food. The blue plate special turned out to be chicken-fried steak with cream gravy, green beans cooked with pork seasoning and brown-sugar-glazed carrots. Soft rolls the size of Trent's fist accompanied the meal.

Annie looked at him comically after Mindy bustled away. "Can you imagine how many calories and fat grams are on this plate?"

"No." He picked up his fork. "I don't care. I'm hungry."

She smiled and cut into her meat. "So am I."

To his satisfaction, she ate heartily. A few extra calories and fat grams wouldn't hurt her this once, he figured. As for him—well, he still wasn't back in pre-accident shape, himself. He hadn't had much appetite during the past months. Tonight he was hungry.

"My grandmother used to make chicken-fried steak for me," he heard himself saying, though he hadn't actually planned to initiate a conversation. Still, it seemed sort of rude to eat in silence. "She died when I was just a kid, but I remember her cooking."

Annie seemed encouraged by the personal tidbit. "My grandmother on my mother's side was French. She made pastries like you wouldn't believe. She promised when I was old enough she would teach me her recipes, but she died when I was only ten."

"Didn't your mother learn the recipes?"

It intrigued him the way her expressive face suddenly blanked. "My mother doesn't cook," she said, little emotion revealed in her voice.

Every time he asked about her past, she clammed up. Withdrew. He kept his tone casual as he asked, "So who cooked for you when you were growing up?"

"Other people," she said evasively.

"I see." He'd obviously stumbled upon a sensitive spot. "Are your parents still living?"

"Yes, but I don't see them often. Tell me about the remodeling project your father and brother are planning. What does Trevor want you to do?"

She'd very efficiently erected a No Trespassing sign

around the subject of her personal life. Trent would honor her wishes—for now. "He wants to replace all the pine cabinetry with a darker, richer wood in a more traditional style. Something more dignified and lawyerly."

"Lawyerly?" She smiled as she repeated the word. "Is that an established decorating term?"

"If it's not, it should be. He said he wants to project an image. Dark woods—cherry, mahogany, maybe walnut—glass-fronted barrister cases, hunting prints and leather. He wants to start around the first of June, which will give me time to do your painting first."

He had already purchased the paint in the color she'd chosen for her bedrooms and hallways. The cans were stacked, along with the painting supplies he would be using, in one of the two small, empty bedrooms in the three-bedroom house. He had decided to paint the inside of the house first, to brighten up her living quarters, and she had agreed with an eagerness that had told him she was tired of being surrounded by dull, dirty walls.

"I know you'll do a great job at the law firm's offices," she said. "Have you considered taking more commissions?"

"Starting a cabinetry business, you mean?" He shrugged. "Maybe. I'll see how this job for Trevor works out. If I screw that up, no one else will want to hire me."

"You won't screw up." She looked amused by the idea. "As beautiful as your work is, I think you'll be in big demand."

It was something he'd been considering for the past couple of months. As his mother had pointed out on numerous occasions, it was past time for him to stop mourning his broken dreams and get on with his life. Cabinetry had certainly never been a career plan for him—but now that the only job he'd ever really wanted was out of the question, he had to come up with an alternative.

His vision loss meant that he could no longer work as a pilot, but the woodworking he'd always enjoyed as a hobby was still a viable possibility. His trick back could prove problematic at times, but if he used reasonable care, hired an assistant for the heavy stuff and gave himself plenty of time for each job to allow for the bad days, he should be able to make a satisfactory living. Hardly a glamorous career—not like jockeying a fighter jet—but it would give him a purpose his life had been lacking lately.

He couldn't see himself working nine to five behind a desk, but being self-employed, working with wood and his tools, seemed like a life he could tolerate. He could take the commissions that appealed to him, turn down the ones that didn't, live simply and quietly— all in all, it didn't sound so bad. If he couldn't fly.

"I'll think about it," he said with a shrug. "What about you? Do you have any goals beyond cleaning houses and teaching kids to play piano?"

"I don't know yet," she admitted. "I've only recently struck out on my own. I've been concentrating on getting on my feet financially. I haven't had time to make long-term plans."

He slipped smoothly past her No Trespassing sign. "What were you running from, Annie? A bad marriage?"

"No. I've never been married." She glanced from

her nearly empty plate to her watch. "I'd better go. I don't want to be late for my piano lesson."

Mindy stopped by the table and set the check in front of Trent. "Can I get y'all anything else?"

"No, that's everything. Thanks, Mindy," he said.

"You bet. Give my best to your family. And next time you talk to that sister of yours, tell her to stop by when she's in town, okay? I haven't seen Tara and that good-looking husband of hers in ages. And I bet their little girl is growing up fast."

"Yes. Alison's walking, and talking a mile a minute these days. Blake's even teaching her to juggle. She should have it mastered by the time she's two."

Mindy giggled. "Sounds like she's as smart as her mama."

"I'd like to pay for my own meal," Annie said when Mindy had walked away.

"Forget it. I asked *you*, remember?" He dared her with his eyes to argue.

Wisely, she didn't try. "Then I'll thank you and be on my way."

"I'll walk you to your car." He rose with her and tossed a bill on the table, enough to cover the meals and provide a generous tip.

He felt the eyes on him again as he escorted Annie out. Again, he ignored them. He didn't even nod to the people he knew for fear of being detained. They'd probably talk about how rude and unfriendly he'd been, but big deal. There was nothing folks around here liked better than talking about the McBrides.

It was just getting darker outside, and a stiff, early-spring breeze put a slight chill in the air that had been pleasantly warm earlier. Proving that she'd learned a great deal about the local citizens during the relatively short time she had lived here, Annie looked up at Trent as they reached her car and said, "I guess everyone in town will be speculating tomorrow about why you and I had dinner together this evening."

He shrugged. "I'm used to being talked about, but I'm sorry if it makes you uncomfortable."

"I didn't say that." She unlocked her car door. "Thanks again for the meal, Trent."

The breeze had ruffled her glossy, brown hair, tossing a strand into her face and over her left eye. Without thinking about it, he reached out to smooth it back. He hadn't planned to let his fingers trail across the soft skin of her cheek, nor to allow them to linger, tangled in the hair at the side of her face. He hadn't deliberately moved closer, so they stood toe-to-toe, his head bent so that their faces were very close together. He didn't intend to get lost in her big, brown eyes—but he did.

It had been a long time since he'd kissed a pretty woman, he found himself thinking. It was something he hadn't given much thought to lately, being so absorbed in his other problems. He was giving it serious thought now.

He saw her lips tremble and knew she must have read the temptation in his eyes. He dropped his hand and stepped back—not from lack of desire or concern about their surroundings, but because he wasn't sure just where an impulsive kiss would lead them.

If she was disappointed, she didn't let it show. She looked quickly away. "I'll see you next week," she said, sliding into her car.

He nodded, then stood where he was while she backed out of her parking space and drove away.

Someone called his name from across the parking lot. He turned his head and recognized a former classmate from high school. Nice enough guy, but a real talker, hard to get away from once he got started. Trent raised a hand in greeting, then climbed quickly into his truck to avoid being caught up in conversation.

THOUGH HE TRIED to focus on other things that evening, Annie haunted Trent's thoughts after he left her. He attempted to watch TV, but couldn't concentrate for worrying about how frail and tired she'd looked when he'd caught her resting in Trevor's office. He made an effort to work on his plans for the law firm's cabinetry, but found himself remembering the sincerity in Annie's voice when she'd told him how much she admired his work. He lay in bed later and remembered her bleak expression when she'd told him she wasn't in contact with her parents.

Annie had gotten to him during the past couple of months. He didn't know how or when, exactly, but somehow she'd slipped behind his defenses. For the first time in more than a year, he was spending more time thinking about someone else than himself. After all these months when he'd been the one being nagged to eat better and take care of himself, now he was fretting about someone else's health.

It must be the vulnerability projected by her slight build and big brown eyes, he mused, crossing his arms behind his head and staring at the dark ceiling. While he knew her fragile appearance was somewhat deceptive, he still found himself feeling uncharacteristically protective toward her.

It was ridiculous, of course, for him to feel this way. He was no hero. He was hardly in a condition to take care of himself, much less anyone else. He didn't know what had happened to leave her alone and near-penniless, estranged from her family, but he knew damn well there was nothing he could do to fix it—even if she wanted him to get personally involved, which she obviously did not.

There had been a time when he would have seen her as a potential conquest. When he'd been attracted to a woman—as he was to Annie—he had pursued her without worrying about where it would lead or what she might need from him. He hadn't exactly kept notches on his bedpost, but he and his academy mates had competed vigorously for feminine attention. And there had been plenty of women who hadn't seemed to mind being trophies in their game.

He wasn't proud of his youthful record with women, but it was a part of his past that was over now—along with the flying, the traveling, the partying with his buddies. The smug assurance that had come with being young and virile and indestructible—or so he had mistakenly believed. He'd been grounded now, tethered to a place where everything he did was watched and discussed, where every action had consequences, and every careless gesture was analyzed for deeper meaning.

Even if he was the same guy he used to be—which he wasn't—and even if Annie was the type of party girl he had once preferred—which she wasn't—and even if she was interested in a fling with him—which he doubted—he wouldn't subject her to the gossip being involved with a McBride would entail. Trevor called it the McBride Curse. For some reason the residents of Honoria had found his family fascinating fodder for dinner-table discussion. Annie seemed to relish her privacy too much to enjoy being in the gossip hot seat. He'd always hated it, himself.

So maybe it would be better if there were no more public dinners. No more near kisses. No more than the pleasantly professional relationship they had maintained—more or less—before.

Definitely the best plan, he told himself, pounding his pillow and settling back into it.

Now if only he could stick to it.

6

BECAUSE SHE was restless on Sunday morning and had nothing better to do, Annie found herself in the spare bedroom where Trent had left the painting supplies. She thought this room would make a nice study, giving her a place to do her paperwork. She could look for a good used desk, and line the walls with bookcases so she could move the paperbacks out of the living room.

The house was shaping up so nicely under Trent's talented hands that she was growing optimistic about how nice it could look eventually. It would take time and money, but she had no other plans.

Her move to Honoria had been impulsive, and she hadn't really intended to settle here permanently, but now she was beginning to think she just might. Despite the gossip, this was a nice place to live. With the exception of a few ordinary break-ins and domestic altercations, there was little crime. The house was hers, free and clear, and the money she was earning cleaning and giving piano lessons could be put to good use.

She was considering eventually opening a studio to give music lessons full time; there certainly seemed to be a demand for that in this area. Cleaning wasn't such a bad way to make a living, but she had to admit she preferred music, and loved working with children. The other spare bedroom would make a good studio; it had big windows and opened directly off the living room. Of course, it would take a while to earn enough to buy a piano. She thought wistfully of the beautiful instrument she'd left behind when she'd moved out of her parents' house. Maybe she could rent one until she could afford to buy, she mused.

Tilting her head consideringly, she looked from the paint cans to the dingy walls of the spare bedroom. Painting didn't really look so hard. Everything she needed was right here in front of her. Trent had so many other things to do—painting the outside of the house was going to be a major undertaking—maybe she could help him out a little and give herself something to do at the same time.

She changed into an old, faded yellow T-shirt and a pair of almost indecently short denim cutoffs that she usually wore for working in the yard. Pulling her hair into a messy ponytail, she slipped her bare feet into canvas sneakers and moved back into the bedroom. She carefully covered the hardwood floor with the clear plastic Trent had provided, and lay an open how-to book she'd recently bought in the center of it. And then she set to work.

IT TOOK SO LONG for Annie to answer the door Sunday afternoon, Trent might have thought she wasn't home had her car not been parked in the driveway. He was beginning to wonder what was keeping her, when the door finally opened.

He felt an involuntary grin spread across his face. And then laughter spilled out of him, coming from someplace deep inside, a place he'd almost forgotten was there.

She looked ridiculous. And utterly, totally adorable.

Generous splotches of paint decorated her face and hair. He recognized the color—it was called peaches and cream. He knew that because he had purchased it only a few days before. He'd intended it for her walls, not her face and clothes.

And speaking of her clothes...

His gaze traveled downward, taking in her tight-fitting, paint-splattered T-shirt and shorts that were just this side of heart-attack length. For someone so lacking in inches, she certainly wasn't lacking in curves. Or legs. Luscious legs—even smeared with paint.

Her hands fisted at her hips, where his attention had lingered. "Don't laugh at me. I've been painting."

"So I see. Um—did you leave any paint for the walls?"

Her lips twitched as she glanced down at herself. "I did splop a bit, didn't I?"

"Yes. I would say you splopped." Dragging his gaze away from her legs, he glanced beyond her. "Um..."

"It doesn't look bad," she said, sounding defensive again. "I was very careful, and I followed the directions in the instruction book."

"Hey, it's your house. Paint your heart out."

She smiled again. "Come see what I've done. And feel free to make all the snide remarks you want."

Did she really think he'd do that? he thought as he followed her to the spare room where he'd left the painting supplies.

She stepped into the room and turned to him a bit defiantly. "Well?"

She'd definitely been working in there a while, he thought, taking in the evidence of paint pan and rollers, several different-size brushes, a few paint-smeared rags and the ladder standing against one wall. Seeing the ladder, he frowned at the thought of her working in here alone.

Despite the clutter, she'd made a good start on the job. Three of the four walls had been scrupulously covered with a first coat of peaches-and-cream paint, a marked contrast to the one dull grayish wall waiting for her attention. Some paint was splattered on the plastic drop cloths, but she'd been very careful. The open instruction book in the center of the floor amused him. He could picture her painting a few strokes, running to check the directions then painting a little more.

"It looks good," he conceded, aware that she was still waiting for his reaction.

She beamed as if he'd just compared her work to Van Gogh's. "You really think it looks good?"

"I said so, didn't I? What made you decide to start the job yourself? I thought Sunday was your day to get some rest."

"I get bored if I'm not doing anything," she admitted. "And I found painting very relaxing."

He moved a little closer to her on the pretext of examining the job more closely. "It's going to take another coat."

"Yes, I know. I've decided to paint the trim a pale cream color. What do you think?"

"Whatever you like."

She propped her hands on her hips and surveyed her work again. "I think it's going to look great. It's amazing how much difference fresh paint can make."

His eyes had turned to her again, though he was trying not to stare at her beautiful bare legs. He was unable to resist reaching out to touch one of the many strands of hair that had straggled out of her ponytail. Paint liberally dotted the strand, as well as the rest of her hair. "Did your instruction book not recommend that you wear a cap?"

"Yes, but I don't have one. I tried to be careful, but when I stood on the ladder and reached above my head to get the top part of the walls, paint sort of showered on me."

He still didn't like the thought of her standing on that ladder, though he wouldn't have minded seeing her on it, stretching to reach the highest places, her snug shorts riding high on her...

Hit by a wave of hunger that shot straight to his groin, he cleared the picture from his mind and spoke in a tone that was gruffer than he'd intended. "You're lucky you didn't break your neck."

"I was careful."

He slid his hand from her hair to her cheek, his thumb tracing a splotch of dried paint just above the dimpled corner of her mouth. "If I'd known you were going to wear a gallon or two, I'd have bought a couple more cans."

She wrinkled her nose. "I haven't looked in a mirror, but I can feel the paint drying on my face. I guess it looks pretty bad."

Actually, it looked delectable. And he was battling an almost irresistible craving for peaches and cream.

"No," he muttered, lifting his other hand to cup her face between them. "It doesn't look bad at all."

A wave of pink tinted the fair skin beneath the paint. Her eyes widened, as if she'd just that moment realized how attracted he was to her. How tempted he was to do something about that attraction.

She had gone very still beneath his hands, her face tilted upward, her unpainted lips slightly parted, her small, perfect breasts rising and falling with her quickened breathing. He wanted to kiss her so badly that he could already taste her. He wanted to press her against the freshly painted wall behind her and touch every inch of creamy skin revealed by her enticing outfit. And then he wanted to strip away the T-shirt and shorts and explore the parts of her that hadn't been exposed to the paint.

Her lips trembled as he stared at them. He had to either kiss her or move away.

For one of the few times in his admittedly reckless life, he chose the safer option. He dropped his arms and stepped back, shoving his hands in his pockets.

Appearing suddenly self-conscious, Annie looked downward and tucked a strand of hair behind her ear.

Trent cleared his throat, still not entirely convinced that he wasn't going to lose the battle of willpower and reach for her again. "Want some help finishing up in here?"

She looked at him again. "What...now?"

He shrugged. "I've got a couple of free hours. Might as well finish this room since you've made such a good start. It's a fast-drying paint. By the time we get this other wall painted, the rest will be ready for a second coat. We should be able to finish everything but the trim today."

"You're sure you don't have something else you'd rather be doing?"

What he would rather be doing was out of the question, if not completely out of his mind. "Let's paint," he said.

Her smile looked almost natural. "Okay. We'll paint. Um—by the way, why did you stop by today? Was there something you needed?"

He'd almost forgotten his excuse for coming over. Maybe because he'd known how lame it was even as he'd started his truck and headed this way. "I, uh, was going to take the measurements of those broken boards at the back of the house. Once they're replaced, I can start getting the outside ready to paint."

He could have taken the measurements Tuesday, of course. He really didn't even need them at all. The boards could be measured and cut on site fairly easily. The simple truth was, he hadn't wanted to spend the day alone. And he had been drawn to Annie's house as if she were a magnet pulling him there.

She moved toward the paint. "I suppose we should get started."

"I'll be right back," he told her, walking to the door as a sudden thought occurred to him.

He was gone only a few minutes. When he returned, he came over to her and smiled. "I've brought you something," he said, showing her the Atlanta Braves baseball cap he'd retrieved from his truck. "Maybe it'll keep you from completely covering yourself in paint."

"I don't want to mess up your cap," she protested.

He settled it firmly on her head. "I've got plenty of caps. This one's yours now."

She smiled at him. "Thank you, Trent. That's very—"

"Do *not* use the word *sweet*."

His growled warning made her giggle. "Okay, I won't use the word. But you can't stop me from thinking it."

He could stop her, all right, by kissing her until her brain emptied altogether. Tempted again to try just that, even though it would probably earn him a slap in the face, he made himself step away from her. "Let's get to work."

"Don't *you* need a cap?"

He pulled a battered Georgia Bulldogs cap from the back pocket of his jeans and tugged it onto his head, pulling the brim low to protect the lenses of his glasses as much as possible.

Trent wouldn't have expected that painting a room would actually be a fun way to spend an afternoon. It had been so long since he'd actually had fun that he almost didn't remember how. But Annie approached the job with such eagerness and enthusiasm that he couldn't help but enjoy working with her. He even found himself using his somewhat rusty laugh again, more than once as the hours passed.

Being with Annie was fun, he concluded, even if they were doing nothing more than spreading paint on her walls.

It wasn't easy concentrating on the work when she was so close. It wasn't easy keeping his eyes on the walls when they wanted to wander in her direction. It certainly wasn't easy keeping his hands on the paint roller and off her delectable legs.

He managed, somehow, even when he ended up steadying the ladder while she stood on it, stretching high to reach the places above her head. He'd tried to convince her to let him do that part, but she'd insisted she wanted to. She'd never painted before, she reminded him, and she was enjoying it. And even though he suspected her real motivation was to protect him from putting too much strain on his back—a direct hit to his ego—he couldn't resist her request to let her have her fun. So, he stood beside the ladder, one hand braced on the side, and focused his attention firmly on the wall instead of on the enticing curves at eye level.

She stretched a bit farther than he considered safe, and he put out his hand to keep her from tumbling off the ladder. "Be careful, Annie. You want to end up headfirst in the paint can?"

That made her giggle again. "I'm not going to fall. But it's really *sweet* of you to be so concerned." She stressed the word deliberately.

He gave her a warning look from beneath the brim of his cap. "You know that word irritates me, don't you?"

Her grin was downright cocky as she leaned against the top of the ladder and gazed down at him. "Yeah? So what are you going to do about it?"

He looked at the wet paintbrush in the pan at his feet. "I could always prove once and for all that there's nothing sweet about me."

She hefted her own brush. "Is that a threat, pal?"

He slid his hand up her leg, something he'd been

wanting to do ever since he'd first seen her in these shorts. He made himself stop just above her knee. "Just take my word for it," he said huskily.

He felt a quiver run through her, saw her eyes darken and her cheeks flush. He didn't know if he should be pleased or dismayed to realize that he wasn't the only one fighting attraction here. Despite the monk's life he had lived during the past months, he remembered how to recognize the signs that a woman was interested in him.

Annie was definitely interested, he decided. But she seemed to be resisting every bit as hard as he was— and for good reason, he reminded himself, reluctantly removing his hand from her leg.

"Ready to come down?" He helped her off the ladder, carefully keeping his touch light and impersonal.

She moved a bit too quickly away from him, then made a production of studying their handiwork. "It looks fabulous, doesn't it?"

He nodded, still gazing at her.

"Goodness, look at the time. You must be starving."

He hadn't realized it until that moment, but he was hungry, actually. "I'll stop for takeout on the way home. Let me help you clean up here first."

She shook her head, her ponytail swishing beneath the baseball cap she had so carefully kept clean while they painted. "You start the cleanup. I'll start dinner."

"Don't bother. I—"

"It's the least I can do after all you've done today. What would you rather have? Pasta or omelets? Carbs or proteins?"

"You cook, you choose."

"Pasta, then. I always take pasta when it's my choice."

He made a mental note of that weakness as he gathered together the brushes for cleaning. He never knew when it might come in handy.

They ate with the scent of fresh paint surrounding them. Annie had scrubbed her face and hands, but hadn't yet showered or shampooed her hair. She'd removed the cap, but still wore the scraggly ponytail and grubby clothes—and Trent still thought she looked beautiful. So beautiful that he hardly tasted the excellent pasta dish she had prepared in an amazingly short time.

Funny how he had once thought she was merely pretty. Had he been blind—or just too stubborn to acknowledge his reaction to her?

He didn't say much during the meal and he didn't linger long afterward. She walked him to the door. "Will you buy the paint for the trim? I'll reimburse you, of course."

He nodded. "I'll pick it up tomorrow. Light cream, right?"

"Right. Thanks again for everything, Trent. I love the way the room looks."

"I'll get to those broken boards this week. The whole place should be painted by the end of this month. That will leave plenty of time for me to get to Trent's cabinets."

"I'll see you at your place Tuesday morning."

"Yeah. See you." It made him feel good just to say the words.

He was halfway home when he realized he was smiling, an image of Annie's paint-freckled face still fresh in his mind. Then his smile faded as he realized he could be headed for another crash, if he wasn't very careful.

ANNIE SMILED BRIGHTLY at Trent when he opened his door to her Tuesday morning. Carrying her cleaning supplies, she passed him quickly and set her things down before turning to him. "I saw that you dropped off the paint for the trim in the spare bedroom yesterday afternoon. I didn't have time to paint, but the color looks as though it's going to be perfect."

"Good. I thought it would work. Maybe I'll get to the trim today after I fix those boards."

He was already moving to the door. Annie was disappointed that he seemed in a hurry to leave. She was hoping they could perhaps have coffee together before he left. They'd had such a nice time Sunday, but now Trent was acting distant again.

Did he regret spending those pleasant hours with her? Was he worried that she was starting to like him a bit too much? She couldn't really blame him, since she'd quivered like a jellyfish every time he'd touched her Sunday, a reaction she hoped she'd managed to hide from him. She had convinced herself that her attraction to him didn't mean they couldn't be friends, which was all either of them was interested in for now. Apparently Trent still needed convincing.

Which meant that she should probably follow his example and keep things professional between them this morning. "Is there anything in particular you need me to do today?"

He shook his head. "Just the usual. I'll see you around, Annie."

"Okay. See you, Trent."

But he was already gone, the door closed firmly behind him.

Annie sighed and shook her head as she set to work. One step forward and three steps back. That seemed to be the progression of her friendship—or whatever it was—with Trent. He was definitely a difficult man to understand. She wondered why she seemed so hellbent to try.

She was leaving his house when she noticed a dark car parked on the opposite side of the road. She paid attention to it only because Trent's house was on a cul-de-sac, and there was nothing beyond it in the direction the car was facing. Was someone lost? Having car trouble, perhaps? She wondered if she should ask, and had just taken a step toward it when the vehicle backed up, turned around and drove off in the direction of town. She caught only a glimpse of the driver—a man with dark hair, no one she recognized.

Shaking her head, she climbed into her own vehicle. The planets must be in a weird alignment or something today, she thought whimsically. Perhaps that was why everyone seemed to be acting so strangely.

ENCOURAGED BY how much better the one room already looked with a fresh coat of paint, Annie began to plan to further redecorate her home. She could already picture how much nicer and brighter everything would look when she and Trent had finished.

Deciding she might like a boldly patterned wallpaper in the kitchen, she stopped by a popular home-decorating store, Intriguing Interiors, on her way home Thursday afternoon, having finished a couple of hours earlier than usual. She'd seen an ad in the *Honoria Gazette* promoting several patterns of wallpaper on a half-off clearance through the end of the month, which just might put it in her price range.

She was browsing through the clearance racks at the back of the store when she overheard a conversation in the next aisle. She couldn't see the speakers, nor did she recognize the voices, but she couldn't help eavesdropping since they made no effort to lower their volume.

"Did you hear about someone breaking into Joe Baker's storage shed?" one woman asked the other. "They got his four-wheeler and all his fishing gear."

"I heard they even took the old fly rod that had once belonged to his granddaddy. Now what kind of lowlife scum does things like that?"

Making a mental note to be more careful about locking her doors and windows from now on—and uncomfortably remembering the car that had been parked so mysteriously outside Trent's house—Annie moved on to the next batch of wallpaper, looking for patterns and colors that appealed to her.

The women continued their conversation. "I'm sure Chief Davenport will find whoever did it. He sure seems to take it personally when someone breaks the law around here. By the way, did you know someone bought that old house on the end of Deer Run? The old Garrett place?"

"You're kidding. Who would want that eyesore?"

"I heard it was someone from out of town. Some guy who likes to buy old houses and restore them."

"I'm sure the Garrett place was nice in its time, but I

don't think it's worth restoring. It will probably cost him more than it's worth just to make it livable."

"Well, you never know. A good contractor can do wonders with those old historic places."

Annie wondered if the unknown buyer would be interested in hiring a very skilled woodworker to assist in the restoration project. Trent could...

She brought her thoughts up short. What was she doing planning jobs for Trent? She doubted he would appreciate her sticking her nose into his business, even if her intentions were good.

She picked up a roll of jewel-toned floral paper and tried to picture it in her kitchen. Too bright? Too busy?

The idle discussion in the other aisle continued. "Weren't the Garretts related to the McBrides somehow?"

"In a way. Josiah McBride, Sr., married a Garrett. Anna Mae. They had the three boys, Josiah, Jr., Caleb and Jonas. Caleb's the only one of the three still living, but the rest of the family certainly seem to be thriving."

"Speaking of which—did you hear Trent McBride's starting to get out again? I heard he had a date last weekend with Annie Stewart, that pretty little housekeeper who works for April Penny and Martha Godwin. They had dinner at Cora's. Burt Woodard saw them and tried to get Trent's attention, but he said Trent wasn't paying attention to anyone but his date."

Annie had frozen in her steps, her fingers clenched white-knuckled around a roll of ivy-printed wallpaper. She and Trent had teased each other about the possibility of local gossip, but she hadn't really believed it would happen. She simply hadn't imagined that the locals would find her interesting enough to gossip about.

"It's past time for Trent to start getting out again. When I remember the way he used to chase around this town, making all the girls fall in love with him, so full of spunk and mischief, it just makes me want to cry. I'm sure he and Annie make a pretty couple. She teaches piano, you know. She's started teaching my neighbor's little girl. I see her from my front window when she arrives and leaves, and she's just as cute as a button."

"I've heard that Bobbie's hoping for a match there. She's the one who introduced Trent and Annie, you know. She's been so worried about him ever since he was in that awful accident and had to quit the air force."

Annie was looking for a hole to crawl into when she was mercifully spared further humiliation by the intervention of the store's owner, who approached the other women and asked, "Have you ladies found anything you like?"

The talk in the other aisle turned to decorating, and Annie was able to slip unnoticed out of the store. She had seen a couple of patterns she had rather liked and she planned to return for them after she'd taken the necessary measurements. Maybe she would be fortunate enough to be the only customer in the store next time.

She couldn't help mentally replaying the women's conversation as she drove home. And she cringed, thinking of how Trent would have reacted if he'd been the one unlucky enough to hear them. He'd have hated it—probably even more than she did.

Things had been going so well between them, she thought wistfully. They had become friends, and she treasured each of the few friends she had made since moving here. She would hate for things to be ruined now by careless gossip that would send Trent bolting for safety again, just when he had started to come out of his unhappy shell—at least a little.

7

IT DIDN'T HELP Annie's composure to find Trent at her place when she arrived. He came around from the backyard just as she stepped out of her car. "Um, what are you doing here?" she asked, her voice breathless because her pulse was fluttering so hard in her throat.

He looked a bit disconcerted himself. "I didn't have anything special to do this afternoon, so I came back to finish those broken boards. It took longer than I expected."

"I see." She swallowed, wishing that she hadn't overheard the unsettling conversation in the home-decor shop. "Are you finished now?"

"I think so. Are *you* through?"

"Yes. I thought I would take it easy for the rest of the day. Someone," she added with a weak smile, "recently took me to task for working too hard."

His answering smile was faint, but looked real enough. "I'm glad you were paying attention."

She slid her hands into the pockets of her khaki slacks, feeling the need to say something else. "Do you, um, want to come in for coffee or something?"

He looked from her to the house, hesitating long enough to make her wonder what he was thinking. When he spoke, his question came right out of left field. "Do you like movies?"

Her eyebrows lifted. "Yes, I like movies. Well, some movies. Why?"

"I was thinking about driving into Carrollton, maybe catch that new Harrison Ford film. I like Harrison Ford. He started out as a cabinetmaker, you know."

Rather amused by his uncharacteristic awkwardness, she nodded. "Yes, I know. He's also a wonderful actor. I usually love his films."

"Great. So, you want to go?"

Was this a date? A follow-up to their dinner at Cora's? Or—she swallowed—a gesture to please his matchmaking mother?

He shoved his hands into the pockets of his jeans when she didn't immediately answer. "It's just...you know...something to do. A way to relax for a couple of hours. It would be good for you."

He made a movie outing sound like a dose of vitamins. Which probably made it easier for her to say, "Okay, sure. Why not?"

He didn't exactly look delighted that she had accepted. In fact, he even looked a bit dismayed. But he nodded, forced a smile and said, "Okay, let's go. If you're ready, that is."

"Just let me run into the house and grab a sweater."

"Sure. No rush. I'll just wait out here."

"You're welcome to come in."

His expression revealed little when he replied, "I think it's better if I just wait outside."

She nodded. Leaving her cleaning supplies in the car, she hurried inside to freshen up and grab her sweater. Even as she prepared to rejoin Trent outside, she asked herself what on earth she was doing. If there was one thing she did *not* need in her life, it was to be involved a with a man who was hauling around as much, or more, emotional baggage as she was.

TRENT COULDN'T have explained what impulse had made him ask Annie to a movie. He helped her into his truck, then snatched his hands away from her as if he'd been burned by the brief contact. He didn't know why he'd even shown up here today—it wasn't as if the work he'd done couldn't have waited. "Idiot," he muttered, walking around the truck and opening the driver's door.

Annie looked up from fastening her seat belt. "Did you say something?"

"No." He climbed into his seat and snapped his own belt into place before starting the engine. He didn't say anything as he backed out of the driveway, but he knew he was going to have to initiate a conversation soon. They couldn't drive to another town, watch a movie and come back home without speaking—although that didn't sound like such a bad plan at the moment.

Annie seemed to find the silence less appealing than he did. "I stopped by a home-decor place after I finished work today. I thought I might paper the kitchen."

Since that seemed like a safe enough subject, Trent went along with it. "Find anything you like?"

"A couple of possibilities. I'll go back when I figure out how many rolls I'll need."

He remembered the way she'd launched into the painting project. "Are you planning to hang it yourself?"

"Yes. There are directions in that how-to book I bought. It doesn't look very hard."

Trent gave her a skeptical look. He'd never hung paper, himself, but he didn't think it was as easy as Annie seemed to believe.

As if sensing his misgivings, she added defensively, "I'm sure I can do it."

"I didn't say anything."

"I know. But I heard it, anyway."

He smiled. "I'm sure you can do anything you set your mind to do," he said, a rare attempt at tact.

"Thank you." She smoothed her palms over her khakis—making him reluctantly remember the way her legs had looked in the denim shorts she'd worn Sunday—and cleared her throat. "I, um, overheard some gossip while I was in the store. I was sort of trapped in a corner and couldn't help hearing."

He almost groaned. "Let me guess—someone was talking about the McBrides." It wasn't such a great mental leap. Someone in Honoria was *always* talking about the McBrides.

"Yes, I'm afraid so."

She sounded so nervous that he tried to put her at ease with a tone that was more casual than he felt. "Trust me, we're used to it. Who was the subject this time? Trevor? My cousin Lucas again? They don't say much about Emily since she married the chief of police, and my sister, Tara, and cousin Savannah don't cause much talk these days since they live elsewhere. Or were they just talking about the McBrides in general?"

Annie cleared her throat again. "Actually—they were talking about you. And, um, me."

He scowled, immediately guessing the subject. "Damn. Our dinner at Cora's last weekend?"

"Yes. I just thought you'd want to know."

He could have gotten along without knowing, actually, but he merely nodded. "The best way to handle it is to simply ignore it."

"That's what I thought. It was just—well, uncomfortable. Considering everything, it's probably a good thing we're going out of town to see the movie, rather than at the Honoria Metroplex. Not that we have anything to hide, of course. We just don't want anyone to get the wrong idea about us."

"No, we don't want that," he said, his voice hollow. He told himself that the local rumor mill wasn't the reason he was taking her out of town. Gossip no longer bothered him. He'd simply been in the mood for fresh scenery. And the theater in Carrollton had more comfortable seats than the one in Honoria.

Even as he mentally listed his reasons, he knew they were garbage. He was taking her out of town exactly because he hadn't wanted to be stared at and talked about. This was the best way he'd known of to have Annie Stewart to himself, and still be out in public where he wouldn't be tempted to try something really stupid.

It shouldn't be such a big deal for a couple of friends to catch a movie together. It certainly didn't have to mean anything or lead to anything, despite his mother's less-than-subtle hinting. Right?

Idiot, he told himself again, silently this time, but no less fervently.

"Maybe I shouldn't have told you about it," Annie murmured, reading the displeasure in his silence. "I

just thought you'd want to know what they were saying..."

He shook his head. "As I've said, I'm used to it."

"What, exactly, is it about the McBrides that people
find so fascinating?" she asked curiously, shifting to
face him as he drove.

Because of his limited peripheral vision, Trent
didn't risk looking away from the road, but he was
aware of her eyes on him. He was also aware of how
close she sat in his small-cab truck, so close it wouldn't
have taken much for him to reach out and touch her.
His hand itched on the steering wheel, as if eager to do
just that. He gripped the wheel more tightly.

"Damned if I know," he said finally, forcing himself
to concentrate on the conversation. "We've had our
share of scandals through the years, I guess, but no
more than any other large family, I'd imagine. It isn't
as if we're rich or involved in organized crime. We're
just...well, ordinary. I don't really see what makes
them enjoy talking about us so much."

"When did it begin? The gossip, I mean."

"Years ago. First there was talk that my great-
grandfather was a horse thief, a tale that's grown even
taller through retelling. Then came the big feud between the McBrides and the Jennings family—that
started during my grandfather's day and I don't know
if anyone still living even knows why. My uncle,
Josiah, Jr., was a mean old cuss whose first wife died
from what most people suspected was emotional neglect. His second wife was believed to have run off
with a married man—a Jennings, no less. That man's
son was murdered a few years later, and my cousin
Lucas, Josiah's son by his first wife, was generally

blamed for Roger's death, though there was never enough evidence to arrest him."

"I see." Annie sounded a bit dazed.

Trent wondered grimly why he was telling her all this. Maybe he felt she ought to know what she was setting herself up for if she chose to further her friendship with the McBrides. With him.

Because he'd come too far to stop now, he went on. "Lucas left town for a while to get away from the accusations. After making a fortune in the computer industry in California, he came home a few years ago to visit his half sister, Emily. While he was here, he got involved with Roger Jennings's sister, Rachel, and—"

"Wasn't Roger Jennings the man Lucas was suspected of killing?" Annie asked, proving she'd somehow managed to follow his rather disjointed tale.

"Yeah. He didn't do it, of course. Turned out Roger was killed by his uncle, Sam—the same guy who'd killed Josiah's second wife and the man she was thought to have run off with, Sam's brother Al."

"Uh—?"

"Long story. Let's just say that Lucas was fully cleared of any suspicion of murder. He married Rachel and they live in California. His younger half sister, Emily, is married to Chief Davenport. Have you met either of them yet?"

"No, not yet, but I've heard they're very nice."

Trent was fond of his cousin, and had a great deal of respect for the man she had married. "They are."

"So that's it? All the McBride scandals? It didn't sound so—"

He cleared his throat, interrupting her. "There have been a few others. Uncle Jonas's only child, Savannah, was the most popular girl in high school—cheerleader, beauty queen, all that. At sixteen, she ended up pregnant with twins. The father was a football hero who refused to take responsibility and chose to trash Savannah's reputation instead. The 'cool crowd' turned on her, letting all the jealousy they'd been hiding come out. They were vicious to her. She and her mother left town rather than stay here and subject themselves to the talk. Jonas had been dead for several years by then and they were pretty much on their own."

"Surely your cousin demanded a blood test. She deserved to get child support, if nothing else."

Trent's mouth twisted wryly. "If there's one thing my family has always had too much of, it's pride."

"No. Really?"

Her tone made him glance at her with a grin. "Are you implying you've already noticed?"

"Let's just say, I'm sure you got your share of that family trait. What happened to Savannah?"

"She told everyone she wouldn't force any man to be a father to her children. She and her mother raised those kids for nearly fifteen years by themselves, until Savannah met and married Kit Pace."

"Christopher Pace, the author and screenwriter. I've heard you have a family connection to him, but I wasn't sure what it was."

"Yeah. She caused a lot of talk again when she married him, because of his fame, but money carries influence around here. She's been regarded much more kindly lately—except for those who are even more jealous now that she's married to a successful author.

Don't ever mention her name to April Penny." He knew April was one of Annie's clients.

"Why not?"

"April's brother, Vince, is the cowardly jerk who weaseled out of taking responsibility for Savannah's twins. April was always jealous of Savannah in school, and now it galls her that Savannah's doing so well while Vince is twice divorced, fifty pounds overweight, living in a trailer and selling used cars. He talks about his high-school football days as the high point of his life, and he still denies being the twins' father, though everyone who matters knows he's lying. Not that it's important now—Michael and Miranda are crazy about Kit, who adopted them a year after he married Savannah."

"They say success is the best revenge," Annie said with satisfaction.

"Savannah made mistakes, but she took responsibility, paid the price and moved on with her life."

"Sounds like a good example to follow," Annie murmured, and Trent wondered if she was thinking of her own circumstances.

He muttered, "Yeah. I guess it is." Now if only he could figure out a way to move on with *his* own life.

After a few moments, Annie said, "Well, I can see there have been some juicy tidbits for the gossips to enjoy about your uncles' families, but your branch of the McBride clan seems perfectly respectable."

"For the most part," he agreed. "My older sister, Tara, was a model teenager, never caused a whisper while she was growing up. Of course, she's only a few months younger than Savannah, so most of the attention was focused away from Tara then. She went on to college and law school at Harvard, then joined a prestigious firm in Atlanta. Her only brush with scandal was a few years ago when she refused to sign off on a questionable deal her partners were pushing and she got fired. A few weeks later, she became involved with a P.I. who put her in the middle of an insurance-fraud investigation that almost got her killed. The case was safely resolved and Tara married her P.I. and started her own small law firm, so everything turned out okay."

"Your brother, Trevor, certainly seems an exemplary citizen."

"Trevor's another overachiever, like Tara. He worked for the State Department in Washington, D.C., for a few years after law school. He moved back here after his first wife, the mother of his two children, was killed in a car accident. There actually was a scandal of some sort connected with Melanie's death—I've always suspected she was somewhere she shouldn't have been, maybe with someone she shouldn't have been with—but Trevor doesn't talk about it. He and Jamie caused some talk when they hooked up—before she moved back to town, she was an offbeat New York actress—but they certainly put most of the talk to rest by the quiet life they've led since they married."

"So now the gossips are focused on you."

Which, Trent acknowledged, was the point of this entire conversation, the reason he'd told her so much about his family. He thought she should know just what being seen with him would entail—just in case they spent any more time together in public after tonight. "Yes. Because everyone else in the family is quietly settled down, the gossips have no one to focus on but me. I can't imagine what they find so interesting, though."

"Can't you?" she asked softly, her tone sounding rueful.

Stopped at a red light only a few blocks from the movie theater, he turned his head to look at her. "You know something I don't?"

"Nothing I want to share with you at the moment."

"Annie—"

"The light's green."

Frowning, he pressed the accelerator. Maybe it would be best if he didn't pursue that particular line any further. He had talked enough about himself for one evening—and there were some things he was probably better off not knowing.

ALL DURING the movie, Annie thought about the things Trent had told her about his family. Her thoughts were so focused on the McBride family history that she hardly paid attention to the story unfolding on the screen.

It amused her that he couldn't imagine why the local gossips were so intrigued by him. Former heart-throb jet jockey turned mysterious hermit—of course they were fascinated. And she had to admit she could see why they found it interesting that he'd been seen with her. She was the newcomer in town, probably a bit mysterious to them in her own right, since she'd been deliberately reticent about her own background. In a town where everybody knew everything about everyone, it had to be frustrating that nobody knew anything about her.

She hadn't intended to cause any waves in Honoria. But then, she hadn't expected to meet Trent McBride.

She glanced sideways in the darkened theater, studying his face in the faint illumination of the flickering movie screen. Fascinating? Most definitely. No wonder people talked...

He shifted his shoulders, accidentally brushing against her. A jolt of awareness shot through her, causing her to swallow hard. Her mind was suddenly filled with images of being alone with him in another darkened room—her bedroom. This was no way, she told herself sternly, to think about a friend. But sometimes, she thought as his shoulder brushed hers again, she just couldn't help herself.

They stopped for burgers after the movie, not lingering long over the simple meal, and their conversation centered primarily around the movie. Annie was glad she had paid enough attention to be able to discuss the plot with some measure of intelligence.

During the drive home, they talked about her house and the plans she had for it. She doubted that Trent was really all that interested in colors and patterns, but he made positive noises while she talked. She watched his profile, noting the way he compensated for his slight vision loss by keeping his attention focused intently on his driving. He moved his head from side to side to monitor everything around him, his eyes sharp behind his glasses, and she doubted that very much escaped his notice. She felt completely safe.

He was such a beautiful man, she thought with a silent sigh. Those beautiful, long-lashed blue eyes. That perfect nose. His firm mouth and chiseled bone structure. Her fingers itched to play in his thick blond hair. Just looking at him made her skin tingle. She remembered how embarrassed he had been when she'd called him pretty. But he was.

"You're staring at me," he said, interrupting her appreciative appraisal.

Trent didn't need peripheral vision, she thought ironically. When it came to her, he seemed to have developed a sixth sense. "I was just watching you drive."

"Do I make you nervous?"

"Not at all."

"If you're worried about my vision, don't be. I've passed all the tests. I'm restricted to wearing corrective lenses, of course, but other than that, there's no problem. I just can't pass flight tests."

He seemed so defensive about his minor limitations. Was it because he'd been such a perfect specimen before the accident that he still couldn't accept that he now had a few flaws? "I wasn't worried about your vision," she said firmly, then turned her head to look out the passenger window, making an effort not to stare at him.

Despite Trent's occasional abrasiveness, which she'd come to accept as part of his personality, she had enjoyed the evening, she decided. It had been ages since she'd been out for a movie and a burger with a man. Probably not since college. Preston's tastes had been somewhat more refined. A symphony performance and a gourmet meal in an exclusive restaurant would have been a more typical outing with her former fiancé. He'd hoped to finance a whole lifetime of such expensive evenings—with her money.

This casual excursion with Trent had been more special to her than any elegant evening she'd ever spent with Preston. Probably because she hadn't chosen to be with Trent just to please her father.

Trent parked in front of her house and turned off the truck's engine. He reached for his door handle.

"There's really no need to walk me to the door," she assured him. "I can—"

He didn't even look at her. "I'll walk you."

She sighed and opened her own door. Someday this man was going to have to learn to listen.

He stood silently beside her while she unlocked her front door. Her hand still on the doorknob, she smiled up at him. "Thank you for this evening, Trent. It was exactly what I needed."

"Me, too." He seemed to be in the habit lately of brushing her hair away from her face. She wasn't sure if she liked it or not—while it was nice in a way, the brush of his fingers against her skin was almost too much sensation to bear. It always made her shiver.

"Are you cold?" he asked, nodding toward the sweater she had draped over her arm.

"No, I—good night, Trent."

It was his cue to step back and allow her to go in. He didn't take it.

His face was very close to hers. She hadn't left the porch light on, so the shadows around them were deep, their faces dimly illuminated by the security light on a pole beside the driveway. The darkness reminded her of the intimacy of the movie theater—only now there was no one else around.

She was abruptly, vividly aware of being alone with

him. She wasn't afraid of him, of course, but she *was* afraid of the way he made her feel.

"I'd better go in," she whispered.

"Yes. You probably should." But he didn't drop his hand from her cheek, nor did he move away.

Her lips were suddenly dry. She moistened them with the tip of her tongue. "Trent?"

His gaze was focused now on her mouth. "I'm trying to talk myself out of kissing you."

The muttered words made her throat tighten. "You are?"

"Yeah. It might help if you would push me away or something."

She lifted a hand to his chest, but instead of pushing against him, it simply rested there, feeling his heart beating strongly against her palm. "I *should* push you away," she murmured, trying to convince herself.

"Yes." His other hand rose, cupping her face between them. His head lowered until his mouth almost, but not quite, touched hers.

The last time they'd stood this way, he'd come to his senses and backed off. Undoubtedly the wisest move, and one he would make again. Any minute now.

Propelled by the fear that he'd do just that, she took matters into her own hands. She tightened her fingers around the fabric of his shirt and closed the distance between them.

She had come to Honoria to make her own decisions. To try new experiences. And she had just impulsively decided that kissing Trent McBride was an experience she didn't want to miss.

She might have taken the initiative, but Trent immediately turned that around. He gathered her into his arms and transformed her tentative kiss into an embrace that nearly singed her eyelashes.

She should have known, she thought, wrapping her arms around his neck, that Trent McBride would kiss like this.

He took a step forward, crowding her against the door, his mouth devouring hers. He was hungry, she sensed, with passion gnawing just beneath the surface of the emotional barriers he'd hidden behind. Trent was a very physical man, and his activities had been curtailed since his accident. She didn't want to think he was taking advantage of the first opportunity that had presented itself recently.

And then his tongue slipped between her lips and she didn't care what his motivation was as long as he didn't stop kissing her this way.

The hands that made such beautiful things with wood molded her body from the curve of her hips upward, dipping in at her waist, shaping the swell of her breasts. She arched into his touch, bringing their bodies more closely together.

He moved against her, and she felt the arousal swelling against his zipper. Knowing that he wanted her sent a heady rush of answering desire coursing through her, making her arms tighten around his neck, her body go heavy against his.

Trent ripped his mouth from hers with a gasp that sounded more like pain than passion.

It took Annie only a split second to understand what had happened. He was so much taller than she was, and he was forced to bend to kiss her. By locking her arms so tightly around him, she had put too much pressure on his back.

She released him immediately. "I'm sorry. I'd forgotten..."

He took a step back into the shadows so she couldn't see his expression. "Yeah. I'd almost forgotten, myself."

"Why don't we—"

"Good night, Annie. See you around."

She'd intended to invite him in, but he was already moving away. "Trent," she said, instinctively reaching out to him.

Without glancing back, he moved toward his truck, his back very straight, his steps carefully measured.

Frustrated by his attitude, she took a step after him. "Trent."

His truck door slammed, cutting off her words. And then he was gone, leaving her staring at his taillights in bewilderment and frustration.

The truck was out of her sight by the time she turned and entered her house. And then she sagged against the door, her body still thrumming from his touch, her lips still aching for more of his kisses. Whatever had just happened between them had been more emotionally powerful than anything she'd ever experienced. And she had ruined it.

She groaned and covered her face with her trembling hands, wondering how she would ever face him again.

8

ANNIE APPROACHED Trent's door warily Friday morning, having no idea what sort of mood she would find him in. Would he be angry? Distant? Surly? Or, even worse, chillingly polite?

He wasn't there.

A note was taped to the door. "Go on in. You know where to find the key."

He had shown her where he hid his spare key several weeks earlier, but she had never used it because he'd always been there to let her in. She knew he'd left earlier this morning because he hadn't wanted to see her.

Bone-deep weariness made her steps heavy as she carried her cleaning supplies into his house. She hadn't slept more than an hour or two the night before. She'd tossed and turned, paced and fretted, and had finally given up on sleep altogether. Wrapped in a blanket, she had watched the sun rise from the rocker Trent had given her as she mentally replayed the kisses that had turned her whole world upside down.

Never in her life had Annie considered herself even slightly psychic. But now, as she struggled with her confused emotions about Trent, she couldn't help remembering her hesitation before knocking on his door for the very first time. She had chided herself then for her weird sensation that her life would change when she met him; now she wondered if it had been some sort of feminine intuition speaking to her that day.

Standing alone in his house, she ran a hand across the back of the rocker that was so similar to her own. The smooth surface and satiny feel of the wood reminded her of how clever and skillful Trent was with his hands. She could still feel those oh-so-clever hands on her body. She could only imagine how much pleasure they could have given her had her clumsiness not brought everything to an embarrassingly awkward end last night.

Did he really think it mattered to her that he had some physical limitations? As many concerns as she had about becoming too deeply involved with Trent, his back injury was not one of them.

She cleaned the kitchen and reminded herself that she'd been engaged to a man who had no softness, no sentiment in him. She had emerged from that debacle with her pride and self-esteem in tatters. She didn't want to go through anything like that again—ever.

But Trent wasn't Preston, a tiny voice reminded her.

Leaving the kitchen sparkling behind her, she moved into the bedroom. The bedclothes were unusually tangled—as if he'd spent a restless night too. She swallowed hard before stripping the bed and spreading clean sheets over the thick, firm mattress. She tried to keep her attention focused on her work, tried to think of this bed as just one of the many she stripped and changed each day, but it wasn't easy.

This was Trent McBride's bed.

By the time she finished cleaning and left Trent's

house, she was exhausted. And she still had a full day's work ahead of her.

It caught her completely by surprise when she ran into Trent at the law firm late that afternoon. They arrived at almost the same time, Annie toting her cleaning supplies, Trent carrying a thick roll of what appeared to be building plans. There was an awkward moment at the entrance when neither of them seemed to know what to do or say, and then Trent reached out to open the door for her.

"Thank you," she said.

He nodded and followed her in.

Trevor and Caleb were standing by the coffeemaker in the lobby. They looked up and smiled when Annie and Trent entered. After a round of greetings, Caleb motioned toward Trevor's office. "We'll have our meeting in there," he told Trent. "Get yourself a cup of coffee and come on in. Annie, when you're ready to work in there just kick us out."

"Feel free to have some coffee yourself, Annie," Trevor added. "Or there are soft drinks in the fridge, if you prefer."

"Thank you, but I'm fine. I'll just get to work."

Trevor took a small step closer to her, studying her face with a perceptiveness that made her self-conscious. "Are you feeling well, Annie? Forgive me, but you look tired."

Aware of Trent's somber gaze on her, she made an effort to smile. "Thank you for asking, but I'm fine. Really."

"You should take it easy this weekend," Caleb advised, his tone kindly paternal. "Get some rest."

She turned her smile on him. "I will," she promised, though her weekend was already heavily scheduled.

Nodding in satisfaction, Caleb preceded his sons into Trevor's office. Trevor followed; Trent lingered for a moment in the lobby, still frowning at Annie. "You look like hell. Are you trying to work yourself into the hospital?" he growled.

She straightened defensively, her chin lifting. "I'm quite capable of taking care of myself, thank you."

"Yeah? You wouldn't know it from looking at you."

She hadn't left her father and Preston only to allow another man to boss her around. "Go to your meeting, Trent. I have a job to do."

Far from satisfied, he spun on one heel and stalked into his brother's office. Feeling as if she'd held her own with him at least this once, she busied herself with her work.

The meeting broke up just before Annie finished cleaning the rest of the offices and bathrooms. Caleb and Trevor told her good-night as they left. Trent followed them out in stony silence. Only then, allowing her shoulders to sag a bit, did Annie clean Trevor's office and call it a day. She gathered her things and headed out to the parking lot, just wanting to get home, find something to eat, then crash.

A hand fell on her shoulder just as she reached the back of her car. She started and almost dropped her gear. "Darn it, Trent, you nearly gave me a heart attack," she complained, recognizing him with a mixture of relief and consternation.

"We aren't finished with our talk."

Annoyed that he was still growling at her—just who did he think he was, anyway?—she opened the trunk of her car and hefted her things inside. "Maybe you aren't finished, but I am. I have things to do."

"Another house to clean? A couple of piano lessons to give?"

"I might even give my car a lube job and rotate the tires when I'm finished."

"Cute."

"Thank you." She opened her car door without looking at him. "Good night, Trent."

He reached out to take her arm, holding her in place. "Damn it, Annie, wait a minute."

"Why? So you can tell me again that I'm working too hard? Kiss me one minute and yell at me the next? I don't think so."

"Will you just calm down? All I'm saying is—"

Stress and weariness combined to make her reckless. "Maybe I don't *want* to calm down. Stop telling me what to do."

"Now you're being completely unreasonable. I'm trying to convince you that if you don't slow down, you're going to collapse. How much work will you get done then?"

"Maybe it is unreasonable," she agreed stubbornly, "but it's my choice to work as long and as hard as I want. I am perfectly capable of setting my own hours and gauging my own endurance. I don't need you or my father or *anyone* planning my life or my hours or my future or—"

His face was very close to hers now. As her voice rose, his had grown softer. "Just because I care whether you work yourself into an early grave—"

"And *don't* say I should listen to you because you

know what's best for me. If you knew how many times I've heard that—"

"Fine," he snapped. "Go ahead and kill yourself. I don't know why I bothered to worry about you."

Annie opened her mouth to snarl back at him, then suddenly froze. It abruptly occurred to her that their faces were an inch apart, that he had crowded her against the car and now stood so close she could feel the angry heat radiating from him. He was perturbed with her because he cared about her, he had said. As a friend...or something more?

Her silence made him study her suspiciously. "Well?"

She wondered what he would do if she just reached out and pulled his beautiful, frowning mouth to hers. If she threw caution to the wind again—the way the new Annie Stewart was prone to do—and kissed him exactly the way she wanted to kiss him right now. The way she had kissed him last night.

"Stop staring at me," he muttered, looking suddenly uncertain.

She lifted her gaze from his mouth to meet his eyes. Probably because she knew how he always reacted to the word, she murmured, "It's really very sweet of you to be concerned about me, Trent."

Behind his glasses, his eyes narrowed while he tried to decide how to interpret her sudden mood change. "I thought I'd proven to you once and for all that there's nothing sweet about me."

"You keep trying," she conceded with a faint smile. "But, despite all evidence to the contrary, you haven't completely convinced me yet."

He laid a hand against the side of her face. He

wasn't smiling. "If you had any sense at all, you'd stay away from me."

"I'm not the one who was lurking in the parking lot for a confrontation," she reminded him.

"I wasn't lurking. I was...waiting."

"Because you were concerned about me. That's very—"

He covered her mouth with his before she could say the word *sweet*.

She didn't wrap her arms around his neck this time, but placed her hands on his chest, curling her fingers into his shirt and pulling his lips to hers. It only took a little accommodation to make it work between them—physically, at least. She didn't know if there could ever be anything else for them, but for now it seemed like enough.

After a long time, Trent slowly lifted his head. "Since I know how you feel about me making suggestions for your own good, I guess I shouldn't remind you again that you really should stay away from me."

"If you did, I'd only have to tell you again that I make my own choices," she replied, her hands still resting on his chest.

He nodded as if he'd expected her to say something like that. "Annie, I think you should know that this—"

Her attention was suddenly distracted by a dark vehicle sitting in an empty parking lot across the street. She didn't know what had made her look that way, but she thought she recognized the car as the one she'd seen on the road outside Trent's house.

Noticing her gaze, Trent asked, "What's wrong?"

"That car across the street—the black one. Do you know who it belongs to?"

Since the vehicle was on his right side, out of his range of vision, he had to turn his head to look. As he did, the car pulled away, disappearing down the otherwise empty street. "I didn't recognize it," he said, looking at her again. "Why?"

Feeling a little foolish, she shook her head. "It's nothing. Just my imagination, I guess."

"No, that's not enough explanation. What's going on?"

"I thought I saw the same car sitting outside your house when I left the other day. The driver sped away then, too, when he saw me looking at him. It could be a different car, I suppose."

His hands tightened on her forearms. "Someone was watching you while you were alone at my house?"

"I didn't say that. I said there was a car that looked a lot like that one parked outside your house when I left."

He was scowling again, but this time his displeasure was not directed toward her. "Maybe we should call Wade."

She looked amazed that he'd even made the suggestion. "And tell him what? That I saw a car? I doubt the police chief is going to waste his time on something so trivial."

"I don't find it at all trivial that someone might be following you around. Do you know who it is? Is there any reason you know of that someone could be watching you?"

"Trent, you're overreacting. Nothing has happened. It's probably not even the same car. I shouldn't have even mentioned it."

"Yes, you should have. And if you notice anything else at all suspicious—if you have *any* reason to be concerned—I want you to tell me, you understand? Do you have a cell phone?"

"No. I'd rather spend the money redecorating my house for now."

He shook his head. "You spend a lot of time driving around town alone. You need a phone for safety reasons. We'll look into getting you one first thing next week."

He was doing it again. Making decisions for her, telling her what she should do, as if she wasn't capable of taking care of herself. Just as too many men had done before him, beginning with her father. Maybe it was her diminutive size that made them think of her as incompetent. "In my next life," she grumbled, "I'm going to be at least six feet tall."

"What are you talking about?"

"I'm talking about your mistaken assumption that I want or need your protection. I want to be your friend, Trent, but I don't need a hero."

The word made his jaw harden. "I'm no damn hero."

She'd stumbled into his insecurities again. Maybe Trent had been treated like a hero at one time—maybe he'd even subconsciously gotten into the habit of thinking of himself in that way—but that had been before the accident. Maybe she should just end this conversation before she put her other foot in her mouth. "I'm hungry. If you've finished lecturing me, I'd like to go home now."

"We could stop at Cora's—"

She shook her head, deciding to quit while she was

at least holding her own, if not ahead. "Not tonight, Trent. I'm really not up to being watched and whispered about tonight."

"Then I'll follow you home. Just to make sure you get there all right. And before you start arguing, remember that I have to go that way, anyway."

She shrugged. "Then I can't stop you, can I?"

His smile was grim. "No. You can't."

She was very aware of him following her as she drove home. He pulled into her driveway behind her, but didn't get out of his truck. He merely waited until she had unlocked and opened her front door, and then he backed out and drove on. She didn't try to detain him. She needed some time alone to think.

Did she really want to fall for a man who was rude, moody, temperamental and domineering? No.

Had she fallen for a man like that? She was terribly afraid that she had.

IT TOOK TRENT a long time to fall asleep that night. He did so only after calling himself every synonym for *fool* that he could remember. When the telephone rang at one in the morning, he jerked awake, his heart pounding as he fumbled for the cordless telephone on the nightstand. Calls at this hour were never good. "What?"

"Trent?" There was a quiver in Annie's voice. "I'm sorry, I—"

"Annie, what's wrong?"

"I—God, I feel like an idiot, but I think someone's prowling around my house. I keep hearing someone at the back door, but I don't see anyone out there."

He was already out of bed, reaching for his glasses and his jeans. "Have you called the police?"

"Yes. There was another break-in at the other side of town, and I was told it would be a few minutes before anyone could get here. They said for me to keep the doors locked and wait."

That was one of the disadvantages of living in a small town, Trent thought with a scowl. The police force was small, particularly in the middle of the night. "I'm on my way."

"Thank you," she whispered.

He hated to disconnect, but he had no choice. "Sit tight," he said gruffly and pushed the button. He was dialing Wade's home number even as he shoved his bare feet into his shoes and pushed one arm into the sleeve of a shirt. Wade answered on the first ring, sounding clear and alert even though he'd probably been sleeping.

Still moving toward the door, Trent quickly outlined the situation. "I'm on my way there," he concluded, snatching up his truck keys.

"Don't be a hero, Trent. You don't know what you'll run into."

"Just get your guys over there." Trent turned off the phone and tossed it in the general direction of a table on his way out the door.

A police car was sitting in Annie's driveway when Trent squealed to a stop there. Apparently, the police had arrived immediately after she'd called him. He jumped out of his truck and ran to her door. She opened it just before he reached it, indicating she'd been watching for him.

"The officers are searching the woods around the

house, but they haven't found anyone," she told him, her voice taut with tension.

He laid a hand on her shoulder, searching her face. "You're all right?"

"Yes. Just shaken. I'm sorry I disturbed you, Trent. I shouldn't have called, but when I heard the police were on the other side of town—and your house is so close and I—"

"Be quiet," he said, pulling her roughly into his arms. "If you hadn't called me, I'd have been furious."

She burrowed into his chest. "I really can take care of myself, you know," she mumbled.

"You did the right thing," he assured her gruffly. "You kept your head, called the cops and called me. That's taking care of yourself."

A Jeep with a flashing blue light on the dash parked in front of the house and a man jumped out and moved toward the porch where they stood. Trent looked over Annie's head. "Hey, Wade. Thanks for coming."

Wade Davenport, the solidly built, tough-faced police chief stopped beside them. "Ms. Stewart, are you all right?"

She pulled out of Trent's arms, shoved a hand through her tousled hair and then tightened the belt of the short plaid robe she wore over blue pajamas. "I'm fine, thank you. You're Chief Davenport, I assume?"

"Yes, ma'am. Can you tell me what happened?"

"Two of your men are searching my property, but they haven't found anything yet, as far as I know."

"Did you ever see anyone lurking around?"

"No. I kept hearing someone—or something, I suppose—moving around the back of the house, but I didn't see anyone when I looked out the windows. When I heard scratching on the back door, I called the police, and then I called Trent."

"I'll go check around and see if I can find my men. Trent, maybe you should take Ms. Stewart inside."

Sounded like a good plan to Trent. "Let us know what you find."

He ushered Annie inside and led her to the couch. "Sit down. If there's anything out there, Wade will find it."

"I've heard there have been some burglaries around town lately, but they've been taking big things. Boats, ATVs, motorcycles—I hardly have anything to steal."

Trent settled beside her and took her hands in his. Her fingers were like ice; he tightened his around them to warm her. "Annie, is there something you haven't told me? Are you sure you don't know who could be following you around, spying on you? It seems too coincidental that this happened the same night you told me you thought someone had been watching you."

She stared down at their linked hands, her face revealing little. "I really don't know who it could be."

"You've never told me exactly why you moved here. You said that you needed a fresh start. Why? What were you running away from? Why are you estranged from your parents?"

"I moved here because Uncle Carney left me his house. My father wanted me to sell it, but I decided to make it my home, instead. My father was furious with me for my decision and we haven't spoken since."

"And your mother?"

She shrugged, her eyes suddenly so bleak that Trent

automatically tightened his hands around hers. "My mother follows my father's lead. Always. I've talked to her by telephone a couple of times, but all she does is try to convince me to 'be reasonable' and listen to my father."

"So there's no reason at all for anyone to be watching you?"

"Not unless..."

"Unless?" he prodded when she fell silent.

"My father is a very...determined and controlling man," Annie said, seeming to choose her words carefully. "It wouldn't be entirely inconceivable that he would hire someone to keep tabs on me—but I think it's doubtful that he did."

"You think your father could have hired someone to spy on you?" he asked, wondering how her family had gotten so far off track.

"I said it wasn't likely. He'd probably assume I'd get tired of living here, or that I'd run out of money and come begging for his forgiveness."

"Just who *is* your father, anyway?"

She seemed to be debating whether or not to reply when a knock interrupted them. Motioning for her to stay put, Trent went to the door. Wade stood on the other side, wearing a wry smile and holding a half-grown, shivering yellow mutt of indeterminate parentage. Behind him, the patrol car was backing out of the driveway.

"I found this guy hiding in the bushes at the back of the house," Wade drawled, looking at the dog draped over his arms.

Annie had stepped close to Trent's side, staring at the beast. "A dog? All that noise was made by a dog?"

"We saw what might have been some footprints in that muddy patch by the back door, but there's no way to tell when they were made," Wade said almost apologetically.

"Could've been mine," Trent said. "I've been doing some work back there the past few days."

"Could have been," Wade acknowledged.

The dog whined in Wade's arms. Trent couldn't help smiling a little as he looked at the mutt. A muddy yellow, it was still barely more than a pup, all ears and feet and tail. It was going to be a good-size dog when it was grown, he figured, eyeing one big paw. Looked as though it could use something to eat.

"Any idea who this guy belongs to, Ms. Stewart?" Wade asked.

She shook her head, reaching out tentatively to stroke the dog's broad head. His tail thumped against Wade's shoulder in reaction. "I've never seen him before."

"Most likely a stray. I'll take him to the pound on the way home."

"He can stay here," Annie surprised Trent by saying. "I'll put an ad in the *Honoria Gazette* and keep him here until someone claims him."

"And what if no one claims him?" Trent asked.

"Then I'll keep him. I could use a dog—for protection," she added.

The mutt whimpered and nervously licked her hand.

Wade grinned. "Oh, yeah, I can see he'll be a fierce protector."

"Someone will probably claim him," she murmured, scratching one floppy ear.

"More likely he's a stray," Trent said, already resigned to helping her build a fence for her new pet. "Where's he going to sleep tonight?"

"In the laundry room? It has a drain in the floor, so if he—er—"

"Which he undoubtedly will," Wade murmured.

"Anyway, he can sleep in there until I come up with better arrangements for him."

"Lead the way to the laundry room and I'll carry your pal," Wade offered.

"I'll show you where to put him," Trent said. "Annie, why don't you get the dog some food and water."

He led Wade to the laundry room, a no-frills, concrete-floored cubicle just off the kitchen. Wade set the dog on the floor, then patted it reassuringly. "Nervous fellow, isn't he? He hasn't stopped shivering since I found him behind that bush."

"And Annie wants to keep him for protection. Wonder who will be protecting whom?"

"I heard you've been seeing her."

"I'm not *seeing* her," Trent corrected coolly. "We're friends, that's all. She cleans for me and I do some handiwork for her."

"I see." Rubbing the dog's ears, Wade looked as though he was trying not to smile.

Annie joined them, carefully balancing two bowls. "I brought food and water. I don't have dog food, of course, but I cut up some left-over roast beef and heated it in gravy in the microwave."

Wade chuckled. "He should like that. Now, I'd better go so you can put this guy to bed."

Trent wondered if Annie's cheeks were suddenly pinker than they had been a few moments before. He couldn't be sure because she seemed to be carefully avoiding his eyes. "I'll walk you out," he suggested to Wade, since Annie looked totally absorbed in watching the dog wolf down the roast beef.

She looked up to offer Wade one of the shy smiles that always tightened Trent's stomach. "Thank you so much for coming, Chief Davenport. I'm sorry you were disturbed in the middle of the night for something as silly as a stray dog."

He shook his head. "You did exactly the right thing, Ms. Stewart. Don't hesitate to call me or my officers anytime you need us, you hear?"

Trent walked Wade to the front door and stepped with him onto the front porch. "You're sure your guys didn't find anything?"

"Just the footprints I told you about—and as we've agreed, they could belong to anyone."

"There's something I think you should know, Wade. Annie probably doesn't want to mention it, but it's been bugging me all evening." Using few words, he told Wade about the dark car that Annie had spotted earlier. And then he added that Annie thought she'd seen the same vehicle before, and where.

Wade's first reaction was the same as Trent's had been. He wanted to know if Annie had any reason to believe someone was following her. Trent told him what little Annie had let him know—that her father was angry with her for moving here and was the only person she could think of who would have any interest at all in her activities.

"But she seemed to sincerely doubt her father is involved," he added, to be precise.

"I'll have the patrol car come by every so often just to be on the safe side."

"Thanks, Wade."

"Tell your lady to be careful."

"Yeah, I—damn it, Wade, stop that," Trent growled as the wording sank in. "Annie and I are just friends."

All he needed, he thought in irritation, was for Wade to start implying things about Annie and him to Emily, who would probably say something to Jamie or Tara. Then word would get back to his mother, who'd immediately start planning a wedding. Couldn't a guy have a woman for a friend without everyone making something more of it?

"Smart-ass cop," he muttered as he went back inside to make sure Annie was okay before he headed home.

He found her sitting cross-legged on the laundry-room floor, the dog's head on her lap. The mutt wore a blissfully goofy look on its homely face—but Trent suspected uncomfortably that he might look much the same way if Annie was holding and petting him like that. "I think you've made a friend."

She glanced up at him. "I feel like such a fool."

"Why?"

"All that panic and excitement—all because of a stray dog."

"I didn't notice any panic—and I wasn't particularly excited."

"Which is why you dashed over here looking as though you just rolled out of bed," she said wryly.

He knelt beside her, making a pretense of studying the dog. "I did just roll out of bed. But I wasn't excited," he lied easily. "Just curious."

"Right."

For some reason, no one seemed to believe him to-night. "Bozo there had probably better go out for a few minutes before you lock him up for the night," he said to change the subject.

"Bozo?"

"In honor of those big feet. I'll take him out while you find an old blanket or towel or something for him to sleep on. Tomorrow, I'll help you put up a pen or a fence or something to keep him in. That's the only way you can make sure he won't wander off or get hurt."

She nodded. "If I keep him—which I intend to do if no one claims him—I'll be a responsible owner. I'll have him neutered and inoculated and make sure he has a safe place to stay. I don't believe in letting pets run loose. Too many get lost or hit by cars because their owners wouldn't take responsibility for them."

Rather amused by her attitude, Trent suspected she was babbling to keep her mind off the fear she'd felt earlier. "I'm sure you'll give this mutt a fine home. You have a rope or something I can use for a leash?" He doubted he could carry the gangly dog as easily as Wade had.

It wasn't particularly easy, but half an hour later Bozo had been bedded down and Trent and Annie were alone in the living room. He knew he should leave—God only knew what time it was, since he'd forgotten to put on his watch—but Annie still looked too pale for his peace of mind. "You should get some sleep," he advised her. "You're obviously exhausted."

"Yes." She twisted her hands in front of her and looked doubtful.

"Are you afraid you won't be able to sleep?"

"I'm sure I will."

Unconvinced, Trent pictured her lying wide-eyed in bed, starting at every sound. "I'll take the couch," he said gruffly, making an impulsive decision. "Got an extra pillow?"

She looked startled. "You're going to sleep on my couch? Trent, that really isn't necessary."

He shrugged. "I'm tired. I can rest a few hours here and then head home in the morning. I've slept on your couch before, you know."

"And you barely fit on it," she retorted, a bit of her usual spirit returning.

"I fit well enough." He didn't even want to think about how his back would feel after a night on the cramped sofa, but he couldn't leave her here alone and scared. He wasn't trying to be a hero, he assured himself. He just thought she needed a friend right now—and wasn't that what he'd tried to convince Wade, and himself, that he was?

She shook her head. "There's no need for you to sleep on my couch, Trent. I appreciate the offer. It's very—"

He gave her a warning look and she quickly amended the statement to exclude the word he disliked. "It's very *generous* of you to offer," she said, "but I'll be fine alone."

She was the most stubborn woman he'd ever met— with the exception of his mother, of course. Couldn't even let a guy do something nice for her without arguing. Losing patience, he dropped his hands on her shoulders and put his face close to hers. "Annie—"

She swallowed. "Yes?"

"Shut up and go to bed. I'll be in here if you need me."

He watched her hesitate a moment longer, obviously torn between pride and anxiety, and then she nodded. "All right. But if you stay, you'll take the bed. I'll sleep on the couch. It's long enough for me."

"No. I—"

"Trent." This time it was Annie who sounded out of patience. "Just shut up and go to bed, will you?"

He might have smiled, had she not been standing so very close, looking soft and rumpled and vulnerable. It suddenly occurred to him that he had just made a huge mistake. Spending the night here—in her bed, no less? Had he completely lost his mind?

9

ANNIE HAD BEEN on the living-room couch less than twenty minutes when she conceded that she wouldn't be getting any sleep. It had little to do with the occasional whine from the laundry room, but everything to do with the silence coming from her bedroom.

She kept picturing Trent in her bed, only a few yards from where she lay. He'd been so determined to stay. He had obviously seen how frightened she'd been when she'd thought someone was trying to break in. She winced when she remembered the foolishly female thrill she'd felt at having him rush to her rescue, looking so strong and masculine and protective. She'd felt so safe when he'd wrapped her in his arms, even though the police had already arrived.

This was no way, she thought with a scowl, to convince him—or herself—that she was capable of taking care of herself.

She would have to reassure him tomorrow that she wasn't afraid of living alone. She'd spent a few restless nights when she'd first moved here, but that was understandable since it had been her first time on her own. It had taken a little adjustment, especially considering that her first home creaked and groaned and rattled, but she'd adapted well, she thought. Tonight was the first time she had been truly afraid.

Apparently, she'd been more shaken than she'd realized by the appearance of that car again near the law firm. Both times she'd seen it, the driver had acted oddly, parking in out-of-the-way places and then driving away after being noticed. She still believed it had to be coincidence—what else could it be? She shouldn't have mentioned it to Trent. It was probably just his overreaction that had unsettled her. But she'd been thinking about that car when she'd heard the noises outside her house.

All that fuss over a stray dog, she thought with another ripple of embarrassment.

Unable to lie still any longer, she tossed off her blanket, swung her bare feet to the floor and sat up. Maybe she should go talk to Bozo. They could whine together.

The bedroom door suddenly opened. Wearing only jeans, Trent leaned against the door frame, crossing his arms over his chest. The living room was dark, so he was silhouetted against the light coming from the lamp in the bedroom behind him. She could see him— and his bare chest—well enough to have to swallow hard in reaction.

"Are you still nervous or just uncomfortable?" he asked.

Although she couldn't sleep, she hadn't been particularly nervous *or* uncomfortable until Trent had appeared half-naked in front of her. Now her mouth was dry, her palms were damp, and her lungs seemed to have forgotten how to function. Talk about overreacting!

She cleared her throat, forcing her voice out past a

sizable lump. "I'm fine. I hope I'm not keeping you awake."

He moved away from the door, taking a couple of steps toward her. "As a matter of fact, you are."

"I'm sorry. I'll try to be quieter."

"Wouldn't make any difference." He stood beside the couch, almost close enough for her to reach out and touch him. She had to curl her fingers inward to keep from doing just that.

Annie was neither slow nor naive. She knew exactly what was keeping Trent awake. She stared up at him, debating her choices—and the consequences. Just how much risk was she willing to take to be with Trent tonight?

"I can't sleep, either," she said after a moment. "And it has nothing to do with what happened earlier."

His eyes locked with hers when he sank to the couch beside her. He wasn't wearing his glasses, she realized. It was only the second time she had seen him without them. For some strange reason, that seemed almost as intimate as seeing him without his shirt.

He reached out to brush back her hair, the gesture a familiar one by now. His voice was a deep, sexy rumble in the shadows. "You should have sent me home."

"I did try," she reminded him. And then she smiled wryly. "Just not very hard."

He traced her ear with one fingertip. "It's not too late."

Placing her hands on his warm, bare chest, she felt his muscles tighten in reaction. She felt the shock of contact run through her entire body, centering deep in her abdomen. "I think it *is* too late," she murmured.

Perhaps it had been too late since the first time she had seen him.

He cupped her face between his hands and scowled at her—so typical of Trent, even when he was seducing her. "You should be running as far away from me as you can get, Annie. I'm a mess—in a lot of ways."

Her eyes had drifted downward, studying his chest in the dim light. She saw his scars, but they bothered her only because of the pain and loss they represented. She knew he carried baggage, but so did she. "That doesn't seem to matter."

His frown had deepened, but she knew his anger wasn't directed at her. "I can't even carry you to bed," he muttered, frustration in his tone.

Her decision made—for reasons she would think about later—she stood and held out her hand to him. "I don't want to be carried," she said, pleased that her voice was steady. "These days, I prefer to stand on my own feet."

He rose and took her hand, his grip almost painfully tight. They walked side by side to her bedroom. Annie wondered if he could hear her heart hammering against her chest. It seemed so loud to her.

Trent turned off the lamp beside the bed, so that the only light in the room filtered in through the sheer curtains at the windows. Washed of color and contrast, the room seemed suddenly smaller. Dreamlike.

Just to reassure herself that she really was awake, Annie reached out to touch Trent's face. He felt so very real. His cheek was hot with emotion, taut with need.

Suddenly she was certain she'd made the right choice. She knew exactly how to get past his momentary hesitation. Imitating his characteristic move, she cupped his face between her hands and rose on tiptoe to kiss him.

Perhaps he had only been waiting for a sign that she hadn't changed her mind. The moment her lips touched his, he moved, sinking to the bed, tugging her down with him. She landed on top of him, and worried for a moment about his back. But when his hands began to move over her, she couldn't focus on anything except his touch.

He was a big boy, she told herself, running her hands slowly across his broad, solid chest. He could take care of himself.

He let his fingers trail down her back, from her shoulders to the curve of her bottom. She could feel the heat of him through the thin fabric of her pajamas. His grip tightened and she shifted instinctively, moving against the erection straining against his jeans. The lower half of her body seemed to go liquid in response, her legs settling on either side of him.

Still feeling deliciously bold, she followed his lead, letting her hands wander over his hot, sleek skin. She didn't know if he'd turned off the lamp for atmosphere or because he was self-conscious about his scars, but she couldn't imagine finding him anything but beautiful.

His beastly moods had occasionally provoked her, but they had never fooled her. For reasons even she couldn't fully understand, she had fallen hard and fast for Trent McBride. She couldn't guarantee a happy ending for them—for all she knew, tonight would be both the beginning and the end of their tempestuous affair—but Trent's kisses had given her every reason to believe that this night would be the most spectacular experience of her life.

And wasn't that the reason she had come to Honoria? To lead a life that was completely different from the unsatisfying existence she had known before? Hadn't she wanted to discover who Annie Stewart really was? What she really wanted?

Tonight she wanted Trent.

He nipped at the skin at the base of her throat and she arched her neck, her fingers buried in his luxuriously thick golden hair. With slow, openmouthed kisses, he worked his way from her chin to the deep V of her pajama top. Her breath caught in her throat when his right hand made a leisurely foray from her hip to her left breast, kneading with a gentle, rhythmic motion that soon had her squirming in pleasure. If he could make her feel this good through her clothes, she wasn't sure she would survive once he'd removed them, she thought dazedly.

His hand grazed her hardened nipple and a gasp escaped her. He lingered there a moment, lightly pressing, tugging, flicking until her breathing was quick and ragged. Only then did he unfasten the top buttons of her pajamas, revealing a swath of skin that immediately drew his attention.

His mouth on the soft skin at the side of her breast, he released the final buttons, spreading the garment so she was bared to him from the waist up. She shivered as a delicious combination of cool air and warm breath caressed her sensitized skin. Still straddling him, she supported herself on her forearms, her head thrown back, her attention divided between the warm, wet feel of his mouth on her breasts and the deep, urgent aching between her legs.

"Before we go any further," Trent murmured against her breasts, "I'd better tell you that I didn't come prepared for this. Do you, uh—?"

"In the nightstand drawer," she informed him, her voice so husky she hardly recognized it. She had packed for all the possibilities she might encounter in this new life of hers, though she hadn't actually expected to open the box she'd stowed in the drawer. Or at least not so soon. Then again, she'd never dreamed she'd meet a man like Trent McBride.

Trent nodded in satisfaction and took up where he had left off.

Annie had always admired Trent's hands and the beautiful work he did with them. He proved now that he'd previously shown her only hints of how truly talented those hands could be.

Sliding his fingers inside the elastic band of her pajama bottoms, he pushed them down her thighs. His jeans were rough against her exquisitely tender skin, the ridge beneath his zipper almost painfully hard. She moved again, pressing herself against him, and was delighted to wring a low moan from him. Trent was always so firmly in control of his emotions. She took a great deal of satisfaction in shaking that control a bit—especially since he was totally destroying her own.

By the time they had shed their remaining garments and were tangled naked together in the sheets, Annie couldn't have spoken a coherent word if she tried. She relied on silent language to express herself, using her hands, her lips and the movements of her body to let him know exactly how special he made her feel. She knew it had been a while since he'd been this close to anyone, but if he had any doubt, any insecurity about making love with her, he certainly didn't let it show.

She loved kissing him. He had the most beautiful mouth she'd ever seen on a man, and she wanted to taste and explore every centimeter of it. He cooperated completely, allowing her total access. She took full advantage of his generosity.

She was absently aware of the few concessions he made for his unreliable back, and she took care not to put any stress on him. The experience was still as spectacular as she had predicted. It wasn't so much the way he touched her—it was the way she responded that made their lovemaking so unique. She'd never reacted so forcefully to another man's touch, had never cared so very deeply that his pleasure was as intense as her own. She'd never felt this powerful mixture of hunger, passion and tenderness.

It was who he was that made the difference. Trent McBride, the complex, unpredictable, flawed, but very special man who had stolen her heart so stealthily that she had never had a chance to defend herself. One day he'd been an enigmatic stranger, and the next he had been someone whose welfare mattered desperately to her. At least it seemed to have happened that quickly.

And now, she thought gravely, gazing up at him as he leaned over her, he was her lover. At least for this one night.

"You look so serious," he murmured, his voice a rough growl. "Second thoughts?"

"None," she assured him. She had concerns about

the future, but no doubt at all that she wanted to stay exactly where she was for now.

"It's not too late to change your mind," he reminded her, though every muscle in his body was taut with need, his eyes glittered with suppressed emotion that seemed near explosion and his arms quivered as they supported his weight above her. Every solid inch of him was ready for release, and he had already sheathed himself in the protection she had provided. But still he hesitated long enough to make sure she wanted him to continue.

This from a man who insisted there was nothing sweet about him, she thought with a tender smile. "I haven't changed my mind. Please don't stop now. I couldn't bear it."

He didn't smile in return, but she thought his expression showed relief. He crushed her mouth beneath his and moved against her, teasing her with shallow probes that only stoked her hunger for him. Restlessly, she lifted her hips, silently urging him to take her, but still he held back, offering only a taste of the pleasure to come.

"Now," she whispered, her fingers digging into his back, trying to press him closer. "Please."

He taunted her with another too-shallow thrust. "Better?" he murmured, his mouth curved against hers.

She groaned and raised her knees in an effort to force him deeper. "More."

His hand moved on her thigh, then slid to the inside, his fingertips lightly brushing against skin so tender and sensitized she gasped and quivered. Her fingers curled, her nails pressing into the pliant skin of his back. "Now," she insisted again.

"Do you want me, Annie?"

It seemed an odd question, particularly now when she was all but begging him, but she answered without hesitation. "Yes. Oh, Trent, yes."

Maybe he'd only wanted to hear her say the words. Maybe he had needed to hear her say his name. Whatever the reason, her broken whisper made him surge forward, filling her so deeply and completely that for a fleeting moment she wasn't sure she could handle all of him. But it didn't take her long to decide that they fit together perfectly.

Trent's back muscles rippled beneath her palms as he began to move. She sensed when his control broke, when instinct and passion took over. He wasn't teasing now, and he couldn't even pretend that he wasn't as lost in passion as she was. His breathing was harsh and uneven in her ears, his skin slick and damp with perspiration. She could only close her eyes and hold on, throwing herself into the whirlwind.

He murmured something against her ear. It might have been her name. Her heart was pounding so loudly she could hardly hear over it.

Release came in a burst of sensation so intense it temporarily blocked all her other senses. She heard nothing, saw nothing, felt nothing—except Trent. And she didn't care at that moment if she never came back to reality.

A LONG TIME PASSED before Annie was mentally coherent enough to think about what had happened, and to try to analyze her feelings. Only then was she able to pinpoint what had always been missing for her before.

She felt...complete, she mused, lying in Trent's arms. For the first time in her life she felt as though she was exactly where she belonged. She didn't allow herself to dwell on the possibility that tonight might be the only time she would ever feel this way.

Her stunned paralysis seemed to last a very long time. But eventually she was able to turn her head to study the man in her bed. Trent sprawled heavily beside her, his chest rising and falling with his irregular breathing. He lay flat on his back, one arm beneath her, his other hand resting on his damp chest. He looked comfortable enough, she decided. No apparent repercussions from their exertion. He actually looked more relaxed than she had ever seen him, she thought with a satisfied smile.

"You're staring at me again," he murmured without opening his eyes.

Her smile deepened as a happy, mischievous mood took over. "I can't help it. You're just so pretty."

He opened his eyes with a mild curse. "Would you stop saying things like that? Sweet. Pretty. You make me sound like a damn pansy."

She couldn't help giggling. It was so typical of Trent to make love to her one minute and snarl at her the next. And for some crazy, inexplicable reason, she simply adored him.

"Trust me, Trent, I have no doubt that you are one-hundred-percent, red-blooded male," she assured him. "I just like to watch you scowl when I use those words."

"You're very easily entertained."

"At times," she conceded cheerfully. She knew she should be sleepy. Considering all the excitement earlier and the fact that it couldn't be far from dawn, it was a wonder she was still conscious. And yet she felt wide awake, her nerves still thrumming with excitement.

He turned his head on the pillow to look at her. "You should get some sleep," he said as if he had read her mind.

Nestling more comfortably into her pillow, she was unable to resist reaching out to lay a hand on his chest. "I will. I'm just enjoying the moment."

He covered her hand with his own. "So am I."

She wished she could read his thoughts as easily as he seemed to read hers. He looked sated and content—but what else was he feeling? More specifically, how did he feel about her? Did he envision any future for them, or had he not thought any further than the morning?

"What are you thinking now?" he said.

She smiled again and shook her head, knowing she couldn't tell him where her thoughts had led. "I'm just tired. I suppose you are, too."

He shrugged. "I don't need a lot of sleep."

The light dusting of hair on his chest tickled her palm. She shifted so her cheek rested against his shoulder. "I certainly didn't expect the night to end this way when we parted at the law office."

A short laugh rumbled against her ear. "I can't say I did, either."

"I'm not sorry, Trent."

His arm tightened around her shoulders. "I hope you won't be."

"I won't," she promised. *No matter what happens next.*

He shifted against the pillow.

"Are you uncomfortable?" she asked. "I'm afraid my mattress isn't as large—or as firm—as yours."

She had refused to sleep on a used mattress, so she'd bought an inexpensive set from a discount outlet. Trent's mattress, she knew from changing his sheets, was a much more expensive one, a worthwhile investment considering his back.

As usual, his tone darkened in response to her casual mention of his comfort—or lack of it. "I'm fine."

"Of course you are," she muttered in exasperation. "And you wouldn't admit it if you were in agony."

Equally predictably, he changed the subject. "I haven't heard the dog whine in a while. I guess he went to sleep."

"He's a sweetheart, isn't he?" she asked, thinking of how trustingly the pup had rested his head on her knee. "What breed do you suppose he is?"

"He looks like a cross between a yellow Lab and a pile of dirty clothes."

Annie laughed and lightly punched his forearm. "Do not make fun of my dog."

"Can't help it. He's such an easy target."

"Careful. I might just sic him on you."

"Is that supposed to be a threat?" Without waiting for an answer, he settled her more firmly against him and said, "Go to sleep, Annie."

Though she wasn't at all sure she could, she obligingly closed her eyes, allowing herself to savor the warmth of him beside her. The steady, reassuring sound of Trent's heartbeat lulled her into sleep.

TRENT WAS STUNNED to find himself alone in Annie's house the next morning. Somehow she had managed to get up, get dressed and leave the house without waking him. She'd left a note for him. "Gone to work," it read. "Help yourself to whatever's in the fridge if you're hungry. I walked Bozo and put him back in the laundry room—I didn't know where else to keep him today."

It bothered him that she had somehow done all that without even rousing him. Usually he was a very light sleeper, waking frequently at every strange noise. True, he hadn't been resting well lately, but he couldn't believe he'd slept that soundly in Annie's not-particularly-comfortable bed. The thought of her going off to work early on a Saturday morning after a near-sleepless night, leaving him completely wiped out in her bed, irritated him a great deal.

He spent a few minutes gazing at that bed after reading her note. The hours he'd spent in it had been the best thing that had happened to him in more than a year. Making love with Annie had been an amazing experience—and he was well aware it had nothing to do with the amount of time that had passed since he'd been that close to a woman. It wouldn't have been like that with anyone else. It was Annie, herself, who'd made the night so special.

The feelings she'd evoked in him both excited and terrified him, leaving him wondering what would happen between them now.

Trying not to think too far ahead, he took a quick, hot shower to loosen his stiff muscles, made use of a disposable pink razor he found in her medicine cabinet, then donned the same wrinkled clothes he'd thrown on last night when Annie called. The least he could do, he thought grimly, was to take care of her dog today while she worked.

After a quick trip to the hardware store for supplies, he spent the rest of the morning building a pen in Annie's backyard. Ideally the whole yard would be fenced to give the dog room to run free, but this would have to do until she could make other arrangements. Bozo seemed happy enough with his new accommodations, especially after Trent set out bowls of water and the dry dog food he'd purchased.

Bozo was a good-natured mutt. He'd probably be a good companion for Annie, even if Trent doubted he'd ever make much of a guard dog.

Maybe he'd build a doghouse this evening, he thought, rubbing Bozo's ears. The goofy animal nearly beat himself silly with his overlong tail. "You really are a clown, aren't you?" Trent murmured, and the dog yipped happily in agreement.

Trent straightened, pressing one hand to his back, and looked toward the house. He supposed he should be going before Annie got back, whenever that might be. He'd deliberately kept himself too busy to think much about last night, but now that he'd finished the pen, his mind was suddenly filled with images and remembered sensations.

He understood now why he had tried so hard to resist his attraction to Annie. Somehow he had known from the beginning that there could be no easy, casual, undefined involvement with her. Somehow he'd sensed that Annie wouldn't just invade his life, she would change it—and the prospect of another change unnerved him.

Bending at the knees, he picked up the metal tool-box he always carried in the cab of his truck. A catch in his back made him wince and straighten carefully, aware that he had made too many demands on it in the past few hours. He could do the work he had chosen, he assured himself, but he was always going to have to be aware of his limitations.

He thought of Annie scrubbing floors and changing beds, hauling around her supplies and her vacuum cleaner and who knew what else, and his gut tightened. She deserved better, he thought bitterly—in a lot of ways.

10

ANNIE WAS DISAPPOINTED, but hardly surprised, to find Trent gone when she returned home late that afternoon. But she was delighted with the dog pen he'd built; as usual, he'd done excellent work. And she saw that he'd bought dog food. She set the bag she had purchased beside it, along with the bone-shaped biscuits, a leash and collar for taking walks, and a couple of doggie toys she thought the animal might enjoy.

She had stopped by the newspaper office to place a notice that she'd found him, but her instincts told her that Bozo was a stray, one of the many dogs abandoned on rural roads every day. Perhaps someone had thought him too big or too homely. Maybe someone had preferred purebred dogs over mixed-heritage mutts. Or maybe he'd just been an expensive inconvenience.

Annie couldn't imagine anyone simply dumping an animal to fend for itself. It had always troubled her to read about the thousands of animals crowding shelters and dying on highways because owners were too selfish to provide secure homes for them.

She had always wanted a dog, she mused, kneeling to pet the happy mutt, but her father had never allowed animals in the house. Too much trouble, he had declared. Too destructive. And besides, he was allergic. Well, Annie had her own home now and if she wanted a dog, she could have one. And she would take very good care of it.

Promising Bozo she would be back soon, she went inside to find something to eat, having skipped lunch to shop for pet supplies. It was so quiet in her house. It would have been nice if someone—specifically, Trent—had been there to talk to.

Remembering the way he'd looked when she'd left him this morning, sprawled with such unconsciously sexy masculinity across her white sheets, she sighed with a wave of pure lust. She would have liked to see him again tonight, though he'd given her no reason to expect to.

As she prepared a quick meal-for-one, she warned herself not to hope for too much from Trent. He'd made no commitment to her last night. For all she knew, he had merely taken advantage of a convenient opportunity. A one-night fling, she added with a hollow feeling deep inside her. She had no reason to expect anything more.

Yet she couldn't seem to stop herself from wishing it had been something more.

THE HOURS PASSED and she was beginning to think Trent wasn't even going to call when the phone finally rang at almost 10:00 p.m. Somewhat nervously, she answered. "Hello?"

"Hi."

"I was beginning to wonder if I was going to hear from you today," she said.

"Sorry I've called so late. I've been busy making more of those little rockers like the one I made for

Abbie. The mothers of some of her friends saw hers and now everyone seems to want one. I wasn't interested at first, so I named a price that I thought no one would want to pay, but I had five orders within a week. Go figure."

Annie was pleased. "I'm not surprised. Abbie's chair is absolutely beautiful. Of course people expect to pay a high price for that sort of workmanship."

"Suckers," he muttered.

"Behave yourself, Trent. Those people admire your work. It's a compliment. And, by the way, thank you for building the dog pen. It looks great, and Bozo seems very comfortable in it."

"I take it you've decided to keep the name Bozo?"

"It seems to fit," she said ruefully, thinking of the dog's amusingly goofy behavior. "I bought a leash and took him for a long walk—well, actually he took *me* for a walk. He's stronger than he looks."

"How did he do on the leash?"

"He didn't seem to mind it—to be honest, he hardly seemed to notice it. I think some training is in order." It occurred to her that Bozo and Trent had a few things in common.

"Good luck."

She needed it—with both of them. "Thanks."

"You didn't see that car today, did you?"

"Not that I noticed. Don't worry about it, Trent, I'm sure it was just a weird coincidence. Those things happen."

"Are your doors all locked now?"

"Every door and window," she assured him. "I checked."

"You aren't nervous about being there alone?"

"No," she answered honestly, still a bit embarrassed that she'd caused such a fuss last night—even though she couldn't regret how the night had ended. "If I hear any noises in the backyard tonight, I'll know it's Bozo."

"If you hear *anything* you can't explain, you get on the phone, you hear? Call the cops and call me. Don't worry about being embarrassed."

Unsurprised by this latest demonstration of his mind-reading ability, she merely said, "If I think there's any reason to call for help, I will. I'm not stupid, Trent."

"I know." He sounded suddenly wry. "You're probably one of the most independent and self-sufficient people I've ever met."

The words pleased her even as they puzzled her. He hadn't made them sound like a compliment, exactly. "Um—thank you. I guess."

"I'd better let you get some sleep. Call if you need me."

"I will. Good night, Tr—" A dial tone cut off her words.

Making a sound of frustration, Annie slammed the phone down and fisted both hands in her hair. The man was driving her insane. When she wasn't thinking about making love with him, she was fantasizing about strangling him. She simply didn't understand his erratic mood swings, or his unpredictable behavior.

He had rushed to protect her last night when he'd thought she needed him. He'd made love to her so beautifully, so perfectly last night. He'd obviously spent hours building a safe place for the stray dog she had taken in. And then he'd practically hung up on her after calling to make sure she felt safe tonight. He was just strange, she told herself.

But she'd gone and fallen in love with him, anyway.

She sank back into the rocking chair as the word echoed in her mind. *Love.* Oh no, surely not.

But she knew herself well enough to recognize the truth when it slapped her in the face. After running away from a father who wanted to control her and a fiancé who wanted to use her, she had fallen in love with a man who completely confused her.

Just what kind of masochist *was* she?

By TUESDAY EVENING, Annie was about ready to track Trent down and hit him with one of his two-by-fours—just to get his attention. He couldn't have held her more effectively at a distance if he'd built a wall around himself. Oh, he was polite enough—for Trent. He'd called both of the last two evenings to make sure she was safely locked in her house before bedtime, though he hadn't lingered long on the phone. He'd left a pleasantly worded note to greet her when she'd arrived at his house to clean this morning, explaining that he wanted to get an early start at her place. He'd accomplished an incredible amount of work today, but he'd left before she'd gotten home. He'd even built a doghouse for Bozo.

But she hadn't seen him, not even in passing, since they had fallen asleep in her bed very early Saturday morning. He hadn't even mentioned what had passed between them.

It was obvious to her that he had retreated in panic. But just how much space should she give him before she went after him? Because she had no intention of letting him get away completely—at least not this easily. The new Annie Stewart was willing to fight for what she wanted. And she wanted Trent McBride. He wanted her, too—if the mule-headed man would only admit it.

When her phone rang just after she walked into the house, she answered it eagerly. "Hello?"

She had hoped it would be Trent. She had never expected it to be his mother.

"Annie, it's Bobbie McBride."

It said a lot about Annie's emotional state that her first thought was that something was wrong with Bobbie's son. "Mrs. McBride—is there something I can do for you?"

"I hope so. The pianist at my church fell and broke her leg this morning. She's going to need surgery in the morning."

Relieved that the call wasn't about Trent, Annie murmured, "I'm sorry to hear that."

"It's a very bad time for this to happen, of course, with Easter only a few days away."

Annie couldn't help smiling at the somewhat aggrieved tone in Bobbie's voice—as if the pianist had deliberately chosen the timing of her accident, just to put everybody out.

Even Bobbie must have realized how her words had sounded. "I didn't mean it like that, of course," she said immediately. "I'm very sorry about her poor leg. It's just that it puts us in such a bind. No one here feels capable of stepping in at the last minute to play the special piece of music we'd selected, but Jamie's sure you can do it."

Easter was four days away. Annie gulped, hoping Jamie's faith in her hadn't been misplaced. "When do you need me?"

"Choir practice starts in an hour," Bobbie answered apologetically.

"An hour—from now?"

"Yes. I hope you have no other plans this evening."

She had planned to sit in her chair with her feet up and stare at the phone, willing Trent to call. Since there was no way she was going to divulge that rather pathetic agenda to his mother, she said briskly, "No, I'm free. I'll be there."

"Thank you so much, dear. Everyone will be so appreciative."

Annie hung up the phone, drew a deep breath and dashed into the bedroom to freshen up and change her clothes. She would deal with Trent later, she promised herself. Somehow.

THE CALL TRENT had been waiting for came late Wednesday afternoon. "Hey, Trent. It's Blake," his private-detective brother-in-law drawled on the other end of the line.

"What have you found?"

Blake chuckled lazily. "It's always a pleasure to talk to you, too, Trent. No wasted time on meaningless small talk or family chitchat. You just get straight to the point."

"Too bad more people don't," Trent said gruffly. He wasn't interested in idle chatter when Annie's safety could be at stake. As independent as she was determined to be, he knew she had been unnerved by that dark car, and utterly terrified when she'd thought someone was trying to break into her house.

The protectiveness he'd always felt toward her had doubled since that night. It felt good to be needed by her—even if it shook him so badly he'd been finding excuses to avoid her while he came to terms with the feelings that had been swirling in him since the night he'd spent in her bed.

Surrendering to Trent's impatience, Blake cooperated. "If Annie's father has hired anyone to keep her under surveillance, he's used someone who doesn't normally operate in this area. If he'd hired a local, I would have found it out."

"Damn. I don't know whether to be relieved or worried to hear that."

"I see your point. If her father had hired someone to follow her around, it would be irritating to her, but not dangerous."

"So what if it's some pervert stalker, instead? That sort of thing happens even in places like Honoria."

"Rarely," Blake cautioned. "It was more likely the coincidence Annie believes it to be, Trent. There are a lot of nondescript dark cars on the road—even in Honoria—and just because she spotted a couple, or even the same one, twice, doesn't necessarily mean she's being followed."

"I know. It's just—well, I have a bad feeling about it."

"I'm the last person to discount hunches. They're pretty much my standard operating procedure. But sometimes they're wrong, Trent."

"Yeah." But he still wanted Annie to be careful.

"There's still the chance that Stewart has one of his

own men or someone I've never dealt with watching your Annie. He certainly has the resources to bring in round-the-clock surveillance from anywhere he chooses, if that's what he wanted to do."

Startled by Blake's wording, Trent asked, "Just who the hell is her father, anyway?"

"Nathaniel Stewart."

Trent's jaw felt as if it had suddenly locked. He had to force the words out. "Nathaniel Stewart—as in Stewart Pharmaceuticals? The man who made an unsuccessful run for governor a few years ago?"

"Yeah. Old Carney was his uncle—the black sheep of the clan. Didn't want to fall in line with family expectations, so he took off. Apparently, his great-niece takes after him. I wonder how Nathaniel feels about his daughter cleaning other people's houses for a living?"

"I have a feeling he hates it," Trent murmured, remembering something Annie had said. Nathaniel Stewart's daughter. He sank into his chair, his shoulders drooping. "Damn."

"I take it she hasn't mentioned her father's name to you."

"No. She neglected to fill me in on that detail." He felt like a fool. Here he'd been telling himself that Annie was all alone, that she needed his protection. That she needed him. The truth was, she could probably buy anything she needed, including a whole passel of bodyguards, if she desired.

"She's not going to like it that you've been digging," Blake warned, revealing an intimate knowledge of women.

Trent scowled. "Then she shouldn't have told me

she was afraid someone was following her. There was no way I could just let that go."

"Look, Trent, it probably is nothing, but you should still warn your friend to be careful, you know? Her father's one of the richest men in Georgia. She's rich in her own right from an inheritance she received from her grandparents. She's living there alone and unprotected while she plays out her little rebellion, whatever her reasons. I don't have to tell you that there are people who would take advantage of that."

"No." Trent squeezed the taut muscles at the back of his neck, trying to decide how he felt about hearing the truth about Annie's background. He came up with the answer only a few minutes after hanging up the phone.

The news had infuriated him almost as much as it had depressed him.

ANNIE'S STEPS were definitely dragging when she got home at almost 10:00 p.m. Thursday. It had been a long day, starting with a very dirty house and ending with a lengthy practice session with Bobbie's enthusiastic, but decidedly amateur, church choir. She almost screamed when someone stepped out of the shadows of her porch just as she reached the front door. "Damn it, Trent, are you *trying* to give me a heart attack? You have to stop sneaking up on me this way."

"You never even looked to see if anyone was here. I could have been anyone."

She unlocked her door. "Did you come to visit me or to lecture me?"

"I came because you didn't answer your phone

when I tried to call. I wanted to make sure you were all right. Surely you haven't been working this late."

She turned on the lights as she entered the house, Trent right at her heels. She ran a hand through her hair, then turned to face him. "I was practicing with your mother's church choir. I'm filling in for the pianist who broke her leg."

"I suppose my mother talked you into that?"

"She asked if I could help out."

"And you couldn't say no, right? Your days weren't quite busy enough, so you decided to take on another job."

She was beginning to figure out that Trent was angry, and she had a feeling it had nothing to do with her getting home so late. Studying the man who had made love with her so beautifully only a few days before and who now looked like a fierce stranger, she said, "I don't mind helping the choir out. They've been working very hard on a special piece for Easter, and it would have been a shame if they couldn't perform because of their accompanist's accident."

"And won't it be a shame if their substitute accompanist collapses from exhaustion during the performance? Because that's what's going to happen if you don't slow down and get some rest."

She almost sighed. "Are we back to that? I thought I'd convinced you that I'm fine. I'm not overdoing it."

He took a step toward her and brushed the backs of his fingers across her cheek. The tenderness of his touch almost made her shiver. "You might have a better chance of convincing me if you didn't have those hollows under your eyes," he said in a low voice. "Or if you hadn't lost so much weight in just the couple of months I've known you."

She winced at that direct shot. Truth was, she *had* lost weight since she'd moved here, a result of so many skipped meals and so much physical activity. She knew she was a bit too thin, but she'd planned to start eating better as soon as things slowed down some—whenever that might be. As for her sleepless nights—those were due more to Trent than to overwork, something she decided not to mention just now.

"I'll slow down after this Easter program. I've already turned down a couple of cleaning jobs. I put them on a waiting list because I simply didn't have any openings now."

Instead of appeasing him, her words seem to irritate him further. He dropped his hand and stepped away, the fleeting glimpse of her one-night lover gone now. "Why the hell are you scrubbing toilets and mopping floors, anyway?"

Stung by the implied criticism, she lifted her chin proudly. "Because I have to earn a living."

His reply to that was a muttered curse.

"Just what is your problem today, Trent?" she asked, losing patience with him.

"*My* problem? Nathaniel Stewart's daughter is unnecessarily working herself to the bone and she asks if *I* have a problem?"

Annie went rigid. "How do you know who my father is?"

"Did you really think I wouldn't try to find out if someone has been following you? You're the one who told me there was a possibility your father could be involved. All I did was try to find out if that was true."

"But how did you—?"

"I called my brother-in-law. Blake Fox. He's a P.I. in Atlanta."

"I wish you hadn't done that. No one here knows who my father is, and I prefer to keep it that way—for obvious reasons."

"I don't intend to take out an ad in the local paper. I won't tell anyone else and neither will Blake, but I would have thought you could have told me."

She thought there was a note of hurt behind the anger in his voice. "I'm sorry—but I knew how you would react. I knew you wouldn't understand why I've been working so hard to be supporting myself. I was right, wasn't I?"

"You're right. I don't understand why you would endanger your health and let yourself get in this shape just to prove a point to your father. Did you decide to clean other people's houses because that would really get to him? Are you trying to work yourself into the hospital to make him feel guilty?"

She shook her head wearily. "You don't understand," she repeated.

"Yeah, well, it's a little hard to understand when you never told me anything. And it's a little hard to watch out for you when you don't tell me what's going on."

Because she knew she'd hurt him, even unintentionally, she tried to speak gently. "Trent, I appreciate your concern, but it really isn't necessary. I don't need you to watch out for me. I left my father's house— years later than I should have—to prove that I could make it on my own. I don't need you to take his place as my caretaker."

His face tightened. "Hell, Annie, I can hardly take care of myself," he drawled gruffly.

She almost groaned. "Trent—"

"I'd better go," he said, moving toward the door. "You know how to reach me if you need anything. And, by the way, there's no need for you to clean my place in the morning. I'm taking the day off. It wouldn't hurt you to do the same."

"I'm sorry I didn't tell you," she felt compelled to say. "It just all seemed so awkward. I know it looks odd, but if you—"

"What it looks like," Trent cut in, one hand on the door, "is that the rich girl went slumming to spite her daddy. Getting involved with an unemployed carpenter might have added a nice touch."

"Surely you don't believe that," she whispered, appalled.

He shrugged. "I didn't say I believed it. I just said it could be interpreted that way. People tend to come up with all kinds of far-fetched scenarios when the truth is kept from them. I should know. I'm a McBride, remember? Lock your doors, Annie—just in case some of those crazy scenarios have merit."

He didn't sound angry anymore, she decided. He didn't even sound particularly hurt. He just sounded...tired. Resigned. And she let him go because she could think of nothing to say to explain why she'd made love with him but hadn't been honest with him.

She crossed the room to sink into the rocking chair. Her head was pounding; she lifted her hands to her temples and pressed, though it didn't help. She had always suspected that Trent wouldn't react well to finding out that she was wealthy, especially as often as he had chided her for working so hard.

She had actually begun to feel guilty that he had labored so many free hours on her house when she was fully capable of paying for his work if she dipped into the trust fund she'd been so determined to live without for a while. She'd tried to repay him with equal hours at his house, but she was aware that she'd been falling behind. She had been trying to figure out a way to reimburse him financially without bruising his brittle pride. Yet she had slighted him, anyway, by letting him find out the truth from someone else. She had never actually lied to him, but she had been guilty of deliberate omission.

She had hurt him, and he wouldn't get over that easily.

Closing her eyes, she laid her head against the back of the rocker and wondered if she should be annoyed with him for having her investigated without her permission. But he had been worried about her, he'd said. Coming from Trent, that was something.

He had just started to trust her a little—enough to show her glimpses of the real Trent behind the defensive shell he'd donned. Would she ever win that trust back?

11

EASTER SUNDAY DAWNED sunny, clear, beautiful. Annie enjoyed the church service, the music, the flowers, the little girls in frilly dresses and the little boys anxious to get outside and mess up their crisp new clothes. Her heavy mood lightened for a couple of hours, darkened only by the realization that reality would hit again when church ended and she went home to be alone with her thoughts of Trent.

Bobbie McBride had other plans for her.

"You'll have lunch at our house today," she informed Annie after church, as if there was no other alternative.

"Oh, no, I—"

Bobbie didn't even seem to hear her. "My whole family will be there and I'd like to introduce you to the ones you haven't met yet. There will be more than enough food, so no need for you to stop for anything. Just follow us home."

"Ms. Stewart's coming to lunch?" Approaching them just in time to overhear his grandmother's brusque instructions, Sam beamed in pleasure. "Cool."

"No, really, I think—"

"Oh, Annie, I'm so glad you're coming for lunch,"

Jamie gushed, coming up behind young Sam. "I've told Tara about you and she would love to meet you."

Annie tried one more time to politely decline. "This is very kind of you all, but—"

Bobbie looked at her watch. "We'd better be going. I have a few more things to do to get lunch ready. Come along, Annie. Don't be shy."

"Yes, come along, Annie. Bobbie has spoken," Trevor murmured in her ear, the only one who seemed to realize that Annie had been given no choice in the matter.

She looked at him dazedly as Bobbie bustled away and Jamie ushered Sam and Abbie toward the car. "I wasn't expecting an invitation to lunch," she said. "I didn't bring anything. And I hate to intrude on your family holiday."

"One thing you should learn about the McBrides," he advised her kindly. "There is always room at our table for our friends. I can speak for everyone when I say we'd love to have you join us today."

Annie was quite sure he wasn't speaking for Trent.

"Besides," Trevor added, "Mother is very grateful to you for stepping in at the last minute for the choir the way you did this week. She has a hard time expressing her feelings sometimes, but feeding you is her way of showing her gratitude."

She didn't see any way to decline now without hurting Bobbie's feelings. She could only hope there would be enough people there that she could avoid a potentially awkward encounter with Trent.

TRENT WAS NOT SURPRISED to see Annie at his parents' house for Easter lunch. He knew his mother well enough to have expected her to bring Annie home, whether Annie had wanted to come or not.

Fortunately there were enough people there to make it unnecessary—if not downright impossible—for he and Annie to be forced to engage in private conversation. To Bobbie's delight, the entire extended family had come for the day. The atmosphere was hectic, with adults talking and laughing and children running and shouting, but Bobbie didn't seem to notice the chaos as she bustled from room to room, barking orders like a maternal drill sergeant, and being obeyed with the same deference. She was in her element.

Trent was sitting in one corner watching the activities—specifically, watching Annie mingling so easily with his family—when his older cousin Lucas sank into the chair beside him.

"Crazy, isn't it?" Lucas waved a hand to indicate the general pandemonium. Having been separated from his family for nearly fifteen years, reunited only four years ago, Lucas still seemed to be adjusting to being around so many McBrides at one time. He and his wife, Rachel, lived quietly in L.A., making a couple of trips a year to Honoria to visit his sister, Emily, and the rest of the family.

Trent nodded. "I'm not used to so many people around, either. A few minutes of peace and quiet would be welcome now."

"So you're enjoying living on your own?"

"It suits me," Trent replied, his amusement fading. He liked to think he had adapted well enough to the curves life had thrown him. There had only been a few problems he hadn't been able to deal with, he mused, his gaze drawn across the room to where Annie stood chatting with Rachel.

Following his gaze, Lucas said, "Annie seems very pleasant, though I haven't had a chance to talk with her yet. I'm a little confused—did I hear Aunt Bobbie say she's Trevor's housekeeper?"

Trent scowled, thinking of how ridiculous it was that Nathaniel Stewart's daughter was being introduced that way. Even though that was exactly what she had chosen to do, he reminded himself, still finding her choices hard to comprehend.

It wasn't that he considered housekeeping a demeaning position in itself—it was honest, if very demanding, work. But he simply couldn't understand why she worked as hard as she did, risking her health and leaving her no time for leisure, just to prove to her father that she could make it on her own. There were plenty of other ways for her to make an independent living—he had no doubt Annie could do whatever she wanted. He still believed she had chosen the job that would most annoy her father.

"Trent?" Lucas sounded a bit puzzled. "Did you zone out?"

"Uh, yeah. Sensory overload, I guess. You were saying?"

"I was asking what Annie's connection is to the family."

"Friend," Trent murmured, studying her across the room. "Annie's a friend."

"Then I suppose that's all I need to know. So, how are *you*, Trent? I hear you've been doing some fairly demanding carpentry work."

Which meant the family had been talking about

him. It wasn't surprising, actually. They all kept tabs on each other, primarily through Bobbie. But it still bothered him. "I'm fine," he said, trying not to speak too curtly.

"You're thinking of starting a carpentry business?"

"Considering it."

"I've always said you did beautiful work. I remember when you were a kid you were fascinated watching your mother's brother Phil work with wood. You got all his tools when he retired to Florida a couple of years ago, didn't you?"

"Yeah. He sold me his whole shop for practically nothing. His daughter wasn't interested in any of it, and he knew I was the only one of his nephews who had any affinity for woodworking, so he wanted me to have his tools. I've set up a room in the outbuilding beside the little house I bought last year and I've been building some things in there. I'm getting quite a few requests lately for custom-designed items, so I think I can make a living at it eventually."

"But what about the lifting and bending involved? Will you be able to handle it?"

This was the older cousin who had taught him to ride a bicycle, he reminded himself. Lucas's questions were motivated purely by familial concern. There was no reason for Trent to take offense—and yet it galled him when anyone reminded him that he wasn't in the prime physical condition he had once taken so much for granted. "I'll hire help for anything I can't handle myself."

Lucas nodded. "That's always been my business philosophy. Good luck—and let me know if there's anything I can do for you."

Trent merely nodded and shifted to a more comfortable position on the hard sofa.

The younger children demanded an Easter-egg hunt after lunch. Savannah's twins, Michael and Miranda, and Wade's son, Clay, volunteered to hide the brightly colored eggs outside while the adults cleared away the remains of the enormous lunch they had all enjoyed.

Trent was beginning to wonder when he could make an escape to the peaceful solitude of his own home. He loved every member of his family, but he'd had about all he could take today. It was bad enough that they so often, if unintentionally, reminded him of how drastically his life had changed in the past couple of years. But the most difficult part of the reunion for him was being so physically close to Annie—and yet so completely separated from her.

Every time he looked at her, he wanted to touch her. Every time he heard her speak, he remembered the sound of her husky cries in the night. And every time he tried to talk to her, he remembered the chasm that had opened between them—in his perception, at least—when he'd found out exactly who she was. A woman who had no need for anyone, especially a flawed former pilot.

Everyone moved outside to watch the Easter-egg hunt. Trevor and Jamie's children, Sam and Abbie, competed cheerfully with Wade and Emily's almost-two-year-old daughter, Claire, and Tara and Blake's toddler, Alison, for the most eggs in their baskets.

Trent was standing off to one side watching the festivities from a safe distance when Annie spoke from behind him. "You've done a very good job of pretending I'm not here today," she said quietly. "If some of the others hadn't spoken to me, I'd wonder if I'd gone suddenly invisible."

Bracing himself, Trent turned to face her. She was wearing a little smile, but her eyes were very serious.

He knew Annie was as upset as he was that there was so much distance between them now. Despite the words he'd thrown at her in anger, he didn't really believe she had become involved with him to spite her father. That wasn't Annie's style. She had fought the attraction as hard as he had—but it had been stronger than both of them.

He just couldn't seem to get past this money thing. Even if he could forgive her for keeping secrets from him—which he could—he couldn't adjust to the sudden difference in their status. It had been easier, somehow, when they'd been more equal in his mind. Both starting life over with nothing, both having something to offer the other. She'd made him feel useful again. Even needed.

But she didn't need him. Why would she? And he'd never had a yen to play the male version of Cinderella. "You aren't invisible, Annie," he said. "I've watched you charming my family all day."

"Your mother didn't give me a choice about coming, really. She practically kidnapped me."

He nodded, having suspected something like that.

The light tone she'd been using suddenly darkened. "I hope I haven't ruined your Easter with your family."

"You haven't." His gaze on her full, unhappy mouth, he pushed his hands into his pockets to keep them away from her. She'd been smiling for the others, he remembered. He hated it that he had taken her smile away.

The look in her eyes was suddenly beseeching. "Trent, I—"

"Uncle Trent! Look at my eggs!"

The high-pitched warning came just a little too late. Running up on Trent's side, beyond his range of vision, Abbie barreled straight into him, knocking him off balance. The ground where he'd been standing was unlevel, and Abbie had come from uphill. He stumbled, making a massive effort not to fall and take the little girl down with him. Hands were suddenly there to steady him—Annie first, and then Trevor, who had sprinted toward them when he'd seen what was going to happen.

It was over in seconds. No one was hurt, and not everyone there even saw the incident. Maybe he shouldn't have taken it so seriously. It could have happened to anyone, he supposed—anyone with limited vision, at least. Trent tried to smile to reassure Abbie that she hadn't done anything wrong and to convince Trevor and Abbie that he was fine. No big deal. Nothing to get all bent out of shape about.

He only wished he could believe those things, himself.

"Nice haul there, Abbie," he drawled, patting her head and nodding toward her basket of eggs. "Better go run find some more before Sam finds them all."

Totally oblivious to the disaster she had almost unwittingly caused, Abbie grinned and ran away to join her brother and cousins.

"You're okay, Trent?" Trevor asked lightly, but

watching him closely. "Didn't twist your back or any-thing, did you?"

"Come off it, Trevor. You really think I can be taken out by a three-year-old?"

Trevor grinned crookedly. "I think this particular three-year-old could take out every adult here."

To Trent's relief, attention returned to the end of the egg hunt. A few minutes after that, he found his mother and told her he was leaving. "I have some things to do at home," he said. "I promised to have a couple more of those kid-size rockers finished this week."

"You have to go now?" Bobbie asked with a frown. "I was going to round everyone up for a game of cha-rades."

Which only made Trent more determined to leave. There had been a time when he'd been an enthusiastic and acclaimed participant in family games. Now the thought of charades made him cringe. "I really have to go, Mom."

Because he knew everyone would try to talk him into staying, he thought he would just slip away qui-etly, without saying goodbye. It wasn't as if he wouldn't see them all again soon, he told himself. They made a point of getting together often.

He almost made it. He'd reached his truck when Annie spoke from behind him. "Running away, Trent?"

He turned slowly, his eyebrows drawn into a frown. "I have things to do."

She stood only a few feet away, her arms crossed over her chest, her feet spread as if in challenge.

"You've been a real life of the party today. And now you're leaving. I have ruined your holiday, haven't I?"

"I told you, you haven't ruined anything. My parents can entertain anyone they want to in their home."

"Trent, please don't leave because of me. I know you're angry with me, but don't let that ruin your time with your family. I'm the one who should leave, not you. You belong here."

He glanced darkly toward the house, from which muted sounds of laughter and conversation drifted toward them. "Trust me, Annie, I feel as much the outsider here as you do, if not more. The Trent they knew—the one they still want me to be—died in a plane crash caused by his own reckless stupidity. It wasn't even a military plane on a noble mission. It was a buddy's home-built experimental model that he thought he could fly just because he thought he could do anything. That guy was so cocky and full of himself that he thought the world was his for the taking. He could do anything. He had no limitations. As for me— well, I don't know who the hell I am anymore."

Her eyes had widened in what might have been distress and she shook her head. "Your family knows who you are. You're the same man they have always known and loved. Just because your circumstances have changed doesn't mean they feel any differently about you."

He blew air through his nose, telling himself he knew his family better than she did. "Of course they still love me—and they feel sorry for me. Poor invalid Trent." Bitterness coated his voice so thickly that even he could hear it.

Distress changed quickly to anger as Annie drew

herself up to her full five feet three inches and looked him straight in the eye. This was the look that had taken him so by surprise the first time he had seen it. The time he'd realized that she wasn't the shy, meek little housekeeper he'd thought her at first. Maybe it was then he had started to fall for her—before he had learned how completely wrong that first impression had been.

"That," she said crisply, "is the biggest crock of garbage I've ever heard. Your family doesn't think of you as an invalid, Trent McBride, and neither do I. The only one around here who thinks of you that way—is you."

He put a hand on the door handle of his truck. "I've got to go."

"Fine. Run away. Go home and feel sorry for yourself. But that won't change the fact that for some unaccountable reason everyone here loves you. *Everyone*, God help us. No matter how many excuses you make to keep us away, it won't change the way we feel. All you're doing is hurting us, and yourself, because you're still punishing yourself for making a mistake. For not being perfect. So run hide, Trent, and make everyone else suffer along with you."

What might have been terror rose up to choke him, compelling him to move. To run—just as she had accused him of doing. If he stayed, he wasn't sure what he would do. He had an uneasy feeling he would do something that would change everything—permanently. And he just wasn't ready for that.

He opened the truck door. "We'll talk later," he muttered.

"Maybe," she said coolly. "Or maybe I'll finally

take your hint and get out of your life. If you're so determined to be alone, I don't know if I can change your mind. Or if I should even try."

The thought of her leaving for good punched a hole right through his heart. He lashed out in panic and pain, reaching out to snag her by the back of the neck and pull her roughly toward him.

His mouth only a heartbeat from hers, he looked into her brown eyes, studying the stormy emotions reflected there. Some of them he recognized. Anger. Hurt. Desire. Love? If he saw it there, he refused to acknowledge it.

"Go back to your daddy, rich girl," he muttered, holding himself away from her with an effort that made his hand tremble. "You don't belong here. You don't belong with me."

He watched her eyes fill with tears just before he released her and turned away. He was in his truck with the engine started before she could speak. He knew she watched him as he drove away. He was so distracted by the tumultuous emotions she had roused in him that he forgot to compensate for his peripheral-vision loss and almost sideswiped a dark sedan that was cruising slowly past his parents' house. The near accident only made him more aware of his shortcomings—and that Annie had been there to witness it.

How could she say she didn't think of his limitations when she had been confronted with them so often? And how could he pretend they didn't matter when he had to compensate for them every damn day?

But as he pressed the accelerator and sped toward the sanctuary of his cottage, he wondered miserably what truly made him less a man—a few physical flaws or the tears he had caused in Annie Stewart's eyes.

ANNIE WENT through her routines Monday with emotionless efficiency. She tried very hard not to think about Trent or the words they had said to each other, but it was almost impossible to get him out of her mind.

She started the day by drinking coffee in the rocker Trent had given her. Before she left for work, she walked and fed the dog Trent had named, then put him safely back into the pen Trent had built. He haunted her thoughts while she cleaned her two regular Monday houses and gave his nephew a piano lesson that afternoon. After the lesson, she drove to the McBride Law Firm to clean the offices of Trent's father and brother. When she finished, she would return to the house Trent had repaired for her, to sleep in the bed in which he had made love to her.

Working alone in the law offices, she finally conceded how useless it was to try not to think about Trent. He had invaded her life so thoroughly that there were reminders of him everywhere she looked. And it hurt every time.

Maybe she should leave Honoria, she thought wearily, meticulously dusting Trevor's office. If there was even the slightest chance that she could put more distance between Trent and his family, it would be better if she went away.

Her money didn't change who she was, or the way she felt about Trent. But apparently it made a significant difference in the way he felt about her. Or was her money only another excuse he had found to hold her—like everyone else—at a distance?

She wondered if Trent felt unworthy of being loved. She didn't fully understand his feelings of inadequacy just because he had a bad back and slight vision loss. She had met many people in much worse physical condition than Trent. He had his family, his youth, his house, a marketable skill—there were plenty of people who would trade places with him in a minute, limitations and all.

Yet she couldn't really blame him for being angry. From what she'd been told, Trent had dreamed of being an air force pilot from the time he was a small boy. He'd been close enough to reach out and touch his dream when he had seen it crumble around him. She could only imagine how devastating that must have been for him.

She'd never had a dream like that. She'd never wanted anything so badly she couldn't imagine living without it. And then she had met Trent and tumbled foolishly into love with him. For a very short time, she had allowed herself to dream. If the emptiness inside her now was a measure of how Trent felt about the loss of his career, then she could understand how badly he had suffered during the past eighteen months.

She ached for him, even as she wanted to punch him for what he'd said to her. *Go back to your daddy, rich girl. You don't belong here. You don't belong with me.* She could hate him for that if she didn't understand so well where his anger had come from.

Maybe she *should* leave. Pack up the few belongings she had accumulated here, put Bozo in the back seat of her car and start over again someplace new. She wouldn't go home to Daddy, as Trent had advised her so sarcastically—she would never live under her father's control again—but she could find someplace else to settle. She could clean houses or give music lessons, whatever it took to support herself. But wherever she went, she knew she would miss Honoria more than she'd missed the house where she'd spent the first twenty-six years of her life. And no matter how much time and distance she put between them, she would never forget the first man she had ever truly loved.

She rubbed a dusty hand across her face, then cursed herself when her fingers came away glittering with moisture. She could handle this without tears, she thought firmly, reaching for her vacuum cleaner. She was tougher than she looked. Trent, himself, had said so.

THERE WAS NO real reason for Trent to drive into town Monday afternoon. No reason at all for him to turn on the street that led to the McBride Law Firm. He knew that neither his father nor his brother would be there. Only Annie.

He wouldn't stop and talk to her, he assured himself. There was nothing left to say, anyway. He would just drive past and make sure everything looked all right.

The dark green car sitting in the law firm parking lot made him change his mind. There was a man behind the wheel, just sitting there watching the building. The guy probably believed he would find Annie alone and defenseless. He was wrong.

Slamming his foot down on the accelerator, Trent made a two-wheel turn into the parking lot and squealed to a stop directly in front of the dark car, blocking its path. He had the truck in Park and the door open before the other man had a chance to react.

The other driver climbed out of his car as Trent approached. He was tall, lean and broad-shouldered. Latino, perhaps, with black hair and polished-onyx eyes. Powerful build—the sleek, wiry strength of a jungle cat—but Trent gave only a passing thought to the possibility that the guy could pound him into the pavement. "What the hell are you doing here?" he demanded. "And why have you been following Annie?"

The dark man crossed his arms and leaned back against his car, one eyebrow lifted in a curious expression. "I haven't been following anyone," he drawled in an accent that was as Southern as Trent's own. "Actually, I'm looking for someone."

"Who?"

The answer took him by surprise. "Trent McBride."

Studying the man with a skeptical frown, Trent said, "You've found him. What do you want?"

"You're Trent McBride?" Without waiting for confirmation, the stranger continued. "I'm Mac Cordero. I'm a contractor and I specialize in restoring architecturally significant old buildings. I've recently purchased a house in Honoria that I intend to restore and sell. You probably know it as the old Garrett place."

Growing more puzzled by the minute, adrenaline still pumping through him, Trent planted his fists on his hips and scowled. "What does any of this have to do with me?"

"Several people in town have given me your name

as someone I should talk to about the cabinet work in the house. I've heard you're good, and that you take pride in your work. That you do things the old-fashioned way—not like the cheap, mass-produced junk you find in most new houses these days. That's why I wanted to talk to you."

Trent raised a hand to the back of his neck, still not entirely convinced. "Why were you looking for me here? This is where my father and brother work. And they've left for the day."

"I was just passing by and I saw the lights on and the car in the parking lot. I figured whoever was still here would be able to tell me how to reach you."

The guy had an answer for everything—but something about it just didn't ring true. There was nothing to be read in Cordero's expression—Trent would have had better luck trying to read a statue. "If I find out you're not being honest with me—that you have been following Annie around, I'll—"

"I don't even know who Annie is," Cordero cut in to say.

"I'm Annie Stewart. Who are you?"

Until she spoke, Trent hadn't realized that Annie had stepped out of the law offices. She moved to his side, her attention focused on the other man.

Cordero introduced himself again, adding an abbreviated version of his reason for wanting to find Trent. "I assure you, Ms. Stewart, I haven't been following you."

She glanced at the dark green car behind him. "This isn't the same car I saw outside your house, Trent. That one was black."

"You're sure?"

"Yes, reasonably sure. And I would be willing to swear it wasn't as big as this one."

A very faint smile curved Cordero's hard mouth. "Satisfied?" he asked Trent.

"Not entirely," Trent answered coolly. "I'll want some proof of who you are before I consider taking on a job for you."

"I have references. Photos of other houses I've restored. A couple of magazine articles featuring my work. And I'll want to see samples of *your work*, of course, before I consider offering you the job."

"Once you see his work, you'll offer him the job," Annie predicted confidently. "Trent does the most beautiful woodwork I've ever seen."

Even after he'd treated her so badly yesterday, she was still praising him. Trent scowled. "If you've been asking about me, you've probably heard that I'm just getting started in this business. I did the cabinet work in my parents' house, in my brother's house and in my own, and I'll be remodelling here at the law offices, but that's the extent of my résumé."

"I'm not looking for business longevity. I'm looking for quality. I'd like to see your work, if arrangements can be made. I have to leave for a job site in Alabama early in the morning, but I'll be back sometime during the first week of June. Perhaps I can call you then?"

Trent nodded. "It won't hurt to talk about it, I guess."

"How can I reach you?"

Trent recited his number, which Cordero scribbled in a small notebook he'd pulled from his pocket. Replacing it, he looked at Trent again. "It was...interesting meeting you both. And now if you'll move your truck, I'll be on my way."

Trent didn't much care for the dry amusement in Cordero's voice, but he merely nodded and moved his vehicle out of the way. By the time he'd parked again and got back out, Annie was already stepping into her own car, obviously hoping to leave without further conversation. He moved quickly to stand by her open door. "Wait."

"I have to go."

"I need to talk to you."

She wouldn't meet his eyes. "I think you said enough yesterday. Please, Trent, I want to go home. I'm tired."

She looked more than tired. For the first time since he had met her, she looked defeated. And Trent was miserably aware that it was his fault. "About what I said yesterday..."

"Don't worry, I got the point. You want me to leave you alone. I assume you don't want me to show up to clean your place tomorrow, and I won't expect you at mine. See you around, Trent. Maybe," she added, and shut the door before he could stop her.

Maybe this was best, he thought as he watched her drive too quickly away. Maybe ending it now, cleanly and without equivocation, was the best thing to do. It was what he wanted, wasn't it? No further entanglements with the confused little rich girl who'd stumbled so inexplicably into his life and changed so much. That way it wouldn't hurt nearly as much when she finally grew tired of working so hard and went back to the wealth she'd known before.

He wouldn't follow her. She was perfectly all right

without him. Hadn't he just made a fool of himself again in front of her, practically attacking a man who'd only wanted to talk about a contracting job? She didn't need his protection, didn't need his surly companionship, didn't need him for anything.

He only wished he wasn't so sure that he very desperately needed her.

12

ANNIE HAD HARDLY walked into her house when Trent showed up at the door. Since she had more than half expected him, she wasn't overly surprised, but she was nervous about opening the door to him. Why was he here? To apologize—or to break her heart all over again?

She didn't know if she could take it again without falling to pieces in front of him, something she'd been trying so very hard not to do. Couldn't he leave her with at least a shred of pride?

"What do you want now?" she asked wearily, blocking the entrance to her house.

"May I come in?"

It suddenly occurred to her that for once, he was being carefully polite and she was being brusquely rude. Since the role reversal didn't seem to be accomplishing anything, she sighed and stepped out of the way, figuring she might as well find out what he wanted.

"Well?" she said when he had closed the door behind him.

He was standing very straight, but she suspected it was pride rather than pain holding him so stiffly this time. She wrapped her arms around her waist as she faced him, trying to read his expression. Since he didn't seem to be in a hurry to say anything, she searched for words to fill the painful silence. "You said you wanted me to go away. Did you come to help me pack?"

"I came to apologize to you. I was out of line yesterday."

"Apology accepted." She motioned toward the door, hoping he would leave before her pent-up tears escaped. "Thanks for stopping by."

"I'm not leaving yet."

She'd been afraid he was going to say that. She nodded resignedly toward the couch. "Then would you like to sit down?"

"No." He took a step closer to her and laid his hands on her shoulders. Something in his eyes made her tremble as she gazed up at him, her heart filled with a combination of fear and longing. "Annie, I— damn it."

He smothered her mouth beneath his before she had a chance to ask what he meant.

The kiss was deep, and so intense it was almost painful. Annie found herself hoping it would never end. Trent couldn't kiss her like this and ever pretend again that he didn't care, she told herself with sudden hope. This wasn't the kiss of a man who really wanted her to go away. Could it be the kiss of a man who was afraid to hope she would stay?

When he finally lifted his head, his eyes were filled with more emotion that she had ever seen in them. She couldn't quite read them, but she thought they were the same tumultuous feelings crashing around inside her. "Annie, I—"

Whatever he had intended to say—and she wanted very badly to hear it—was interrupted by a heavy knocking on the door. Trent's head went around sharply, reminding her for all the world of a guard dog hearing a suspicious noise. Nothing at all like poor Bozo, of course, who was more likely to hide and quiver in response to the first scary sound.

"Maybe I'd better get that," Trent said, dropping his hands. "You stay here until I find out who it is."

"It's my door. I'll answer it," she answered firmly, determined to convince him that she could take care of herself. His protectiveness was—well, it was sweet— but before they went any further, she had to break him of this bad habit of telling her what to do. "Why don't you make a pot of coffee, and check on Bozo. We'll talk after I find out who's at the door."

He hesitated a moment, then reluctantly moved toward the kitchen. Tougher than she looked, Annie reminded herself in satisfaction. But when she opened the door and saw the three people standing on the other side, she could only hope she was as tough as she needed to be.

Immaculately attired in a hand-tailored suit, Nathaniel Stewart studied Annie with a grimace of distaste. "I must say you look the part of a housekeeper. Where did you find those clothes—at a thrift store?"

"You've lost so much weight, Annie," Mona Stewart fretted, wringing her hands in a characteristically nervous gesture. "I knew I was right to be worried about you living alone this way. Have you not been able to afford food?"

"How can you stand living in this dump out in the middle of nowhere?" Preston Dixon asked, looking around with an elegant sneer. "Why would you choose to stay here for four long months when you could have been living in your own beautiful home?"

"This *is* my home," Annie told him flatly. "The house you're talking about belongs to my parents."

They didn't wait to be invited inside, but filed past her, looking around as if in fear that something might crawl on them. Annie resented that; her house might not ever be featured in a home-and-gardens magazine, but it was spotlessly clean.

She placed her hands on her hips and frowned at her uninvited guests. "It might have been nice if you had called before you came, Mother, Dad. As for you, Preston, I can't imagine why you're here. You and I have nothing to say to each other."

He gave her the sort of smile a kindly, patient uncle might have given a favorite, but misbehaving niece. He'd looked at her that way frequently when they'd been engaged. She'd hated it then, too. "Now, Annie, it's apparent that your little experiment in independence hasn't worked out exactly as you planned. You're obviously exhausted, you look positively haggard, and this house is little more than a shack. We're all impressed that you've made it four months on your own, but it's time for you to come home now."

"Yes, Annie, you've proven your point," Nathaniel added, speaking with a forced gentleness probably intended to prove that he'd forgiven the harsh words she'd spoken to him the day she'd left his house. "You've shown us you can support yourself, if necessary. We got the message. Now pack a bag and let us take you home—if you have anything here worth taking with you."

"We love you, Annie," Mona said, the perfunctory

warmth in her voice barely reflected in her perpetually vague eyes. "Preston adores you. Let him take care of you."

"I don't need Preston—or anyone—to take care of me, Mother. And what Preston adores is our money, not me. I don't know why you and Dad can't, or won't, see that."

"That's both an insulting and an absurd accusation, Annette," Nathaniel chided sternly, his uncharacteristic tolerance slipping. "Preston can have any woman in our social circle that he wants—"

"Can and has," Annie murmured, thinking of the affairs she had learned about through a jealous ex-friend Preston had romanced and dumped.

Nathaniel ignored her. "You're the one Preston asked to be his wife because the two of you are so obviously well suited."

"Because he thought I was such a doormat that I wouldn't interfere with anything he did," Annie countered. And she had been a doormat, damn it, she remembered with a wince. Until the day she'd finally realized she'd had more than enough of other people's footprints on her back.

Her father frowned heavily at her. "I'm losing all patience with you, Annette. I have no intention of allowing you to continue to throw your life away. You've had your rebellion. You've purposely humiliated all of us by posing as a penniless housekeeper in this hick town. But it's time for it to stop now. We've come to take you home. Get your things and come along."

It had taken Annie twenty-six years to work up the courage to look her intimidating father in the eye and defy him. It was easier now than it had been four months ago—the day she had declared her independence for the first time. "I'm staying right here."

Mona drew in a sharp breath, clearly appalled that anyone could so openly flout the man *she* hadn't challenged in thirty years of marriage. "Annie, please. Can't you see we only want what's best for you?"

"I think Annie is perfectly capable of deciding what's best for her."

Trent's comment drew everyone's attention to the kitchen doorway, where he leaned in a casual pose against the door frame. He looked strong and fit and gorgeous, Annie thought, studying him with the admittedly biased perspective of someone who loved him. His slightly shaggy, dark gold hair was tousled appealingly around his handsome face, and his eyes were very clear and blue behind the glasses that suited him so well. Lean muscles rippled beneath his workman's plaid shirt and worn-soft jeans. She would choose Trent's simple, masculine style over Preston's designer-clad, moussed-and-blow-dried facade any time.

Preston's carefully maintained smile of forbearance faded. "Who the hell are you?"

MAINTAINING HIS relaxed pose with an effort, Trent took his time studying the other man. He'd been shamelessly eavesdropping on the conversation from the kitchen and he'd learned a great deal about Annie's relationship with her parents. No wonder she'd been so adamant about being on her own. Making her own way. These people talked to her as if she were a child. Apparently, they'd even chosen a mate for her.

What kind of parents could be so clueless about their own daughter?

He finally answered the other guy's question with a lazy drawl intended to irritate. "I'm Trent McBride. Annie's...friend. Who the hell are *you?*"

"Preston Dixon. Annie's fiancé."

Trent's chuckle probably caught Dixon by surprise. "Oh, I don't think so," he murmured, glancing at Annie's furious expression.

Annie nodded at him. "You're right. He's not."

Her father had already studied Trent and written him off as insignificant. "This is a family meeting, young man. It would be best if you leave now."

Trent had no intention of going anywhere, of course, but he was pleased when Annie moved quickly to his side. "Trent is an *invited* guest in my home. He's welcome to stay as long as he likes."

It seemed to him as good a time as any to make their relationship clear—to the others, and maybe to Annie, herself. "And if I'd like to stay the whole night?" he asked her, keeping his tone mildly amused.

She didn't even hesitate. "You'd be welcome to do that, too," she said quietly. "After all, it wouldn't be the first time."

A surge of satisfaction filled him, and he smiled at her. Annie had proven that she could take care of herself, he mused. But it seemed she had found a place for him in her life, after all. Right beside her.

Her self-proclaimed fiancé began to look suddenly less confident. He studied Trent's faded jeans and worn work shirt with a slight sneer. "Is this another part of your temper tantrum, Annie? An affair with this guy? This—this—"

"Carpenter," Trent supplied affably. Proudly. "Slightly battered, but still functional."

Annie's smile deepened in response to his laconic self-description. She seemed to approve.

"Oh, Annie, don't do this," her mother wailed, wringing her hands. "This isn't the life you were raised for. We have so much more to offer than you can find here." The distressed look she gave Trent included him in the less-than-desirable offerings of Honoria.

Trent responded before Annie had a chance. Because this woman was Annie's mother, he tried to speak candidly, but not too harshly. "A few days ago—maybe even a few hours ago—I might've agreed with you, ma'am. I couldn't see why Annie would walk away from a life of luxury to work so hard and live so frugally. Now that I've heard the way you people talk to her, I can understand her choices."

"You don't really think she'll be content to stay here long, do you?" Dixon asked with a sharp laugh. "Can't you see she's using you to punish us? Why else would she be scrubbing floors for a living when she has the brains and skills to take an executive position if she chooses?"

Annie huffed inelegantly. "As if any corporation in this state—or any surrounding state, for that matter—would hire me if Dad put out the word that he didn't want them to. Cleaning houses is one thing I can do on my own, without interference from any of you. It's honest work, I'm my own boss, I set my own rates and hours, and I choose my own clients. For the first time in my life, I'm making my own decisions, without consulting you—or anyone. And I like it."

"How well will you like it if you have no other options?" Nathaniel asked shrewdly. "If I cut you off completely?"

Trent watched as Annie's chin lifted in a gesture that reminded him a bit of her father. She probably wouldn't appreciate the comparison just then. "You can't touch the money I inherited from Grandmother Stewart, just as you had no control over this property Uncle Carney left me."

"Your grandmother left you a comfortable nest egg, but it's nothing compared to what you had when you lived at home," her father replied. "How long do you expect it to last?"

She shrugged. "I haven't even touched it yet, I haven't needed to. But it's mine if I ever need it."

"I bet your new boyfriend wouldn't mind helping you spend it," Dixon muttered.

Trent would have dearly loved to cram the jerk's pretty capped teeth right down his throat. He was considering trying when Annie suddenly surprised him with a laugh.

Looking at Dixon, she shook her head. "It's obvious that you've only just met Trent McBride. This is a man who would starve before he would touch a penny of my money. Unlike you, I might add, with your not-so-secret fear that you might starve *without* my money."

Dixon's expression turned ugly. "You little—"

Trent straightened away from the door frame, his hand already clenching in preparation for contact with the other guy's mouth. "I wouldn't finish that sentence, if I were you."

He felt Annie's hand fall quickly on his arm, her fingers tightening to hold him beside her. "I can handle this, Trent," she reminded him.

He gave her a look, his tone wry. "I know. But couldn't I punch him once, just because I don't like him?"

"Behave yourself," she murmured, looking pleased that he had agreed she could handle the situation. And maybe just a little pleased that he wanted to punch Preston for her, Trent thought with a slight smile.

"This is becoming tiresome," Nathaniel announced, and then looked at Annie with what might have been just a hint of entreaty in his dark eyes that looked very much like hers. "Come home with us, Annie. Don't break up the family."

Low blow, Trent thought. Was this the way they had controlled her for so long? By playing on the soft heart he had recognized in her from the beginning?

"The family broke up a long time ago, Dad," she answered sadly. "It happened when I grew old enough to start thinking for myself. It just took us all a long time to finally admit it."

"And if I threaten to take you out of my will?"

"It wouldn't make any difference. Adopt Preston, if you like. And then watch how quickly he slaps you into a retirement home as soon as you're too old to take care of yourself. Preston's very good at being and saying everything you want—as I found out for myself—but when you look deeper, if you ever bother, you'll find that it's all about what *he* wants."

"Your parents know me better than that," Dixon said, regaining his smug composure with a visible effort. Again, Trent's fingers twitched with an urge to rearrange his smile. Funny, he'd never considered himself a particularly aggressive man—until he'd found himself feeling so protective toward Annie, anyway.

"Unfortunately, they don't," Annie answered in regret. And then she turned to Nathaniel again, effectively dismissing Preston Dixon. "You're my father and I love you because of that," she said quietly. "I don't want your money or your guidance, but I have always wanted your respect and acceptance. If you ever decide you can give me those things without demanding total obedience in return, I hope you'll call me. Perhaps we can figure out a way to start over."

"I will never accept that you've chosen to waste your life here," her father answered stiffly. "I gave you every opportunity to make something of yourself, and you've chosen instead to throw it all back in my face."

Looking disappointed, but not really surprised, Annie nodded. "I'm sorry you feel that way. If you ever change your mind, I'm willing to talk. Mother, you have my number. Use it whenever you like."

Mona glanced nervously from her daughter to her husband. "I'll call you," she whispered.

Dixon was still having trouble getting the message. "You're giving up everything we could have had together?" he asked Annie incredulously, then motioned toward Trent with open contempt. "For *him?*"

"No," Annie replied, her fingers tightening warningly on Trent's arm again. "I'm giving it up for me. Trent," she added, smiling up at him, "is a very nice bonus."

Ignoring the others, Trent reached out to snag the back of her neck and pull her toward him for a quick kiss. "Thanks," he murmured when he released her.

"I'm not going to stand around and watch this." Dixon spun angrily on one heel and marched toward the door. Trent watched him leave with great satisfaction.

Annie's father followed. "Neither am I. Annie, if you come to your senses, come home. If not, I hope you're happy here." But he didn't sound as if he really hoped that, at all.

Annie's mother hesitated, looking from her daughter to the doorway, and then moved after her husband. "I'll call," she promised on the way out.

The snap of the door closing behind them sounded unfortunately final.

"Have you ever noticed," Trent asked thoughtfully, looking after them, his arm wrapped bracingly around Annie's shoulders, "that your father tends to talk in clichés?"

"Yes, I've noticed." She straightened her shoulders and turned to face him. "Actually, I first started to question my relationship with Preston when I realized that he had the same annoying habit."

"You were actually engaged to that jerk?"

She grimaced. "Let's just call it temporary insanity and let it go at that."

He wanted to see her smile again, wanted to do something to ease the sadness in her eyes. He kept his tone deliberately wistful when he said, "I wish you'd have let me punch him. I'm sure I could have taken him."

"With one hand tied behind your back," she assured him. "But he isn't worth it, Trent."

He dropped the light tone, placing his hands on her shoulders. "I'm sorry about your parents, Annie. It must have hurt very badly to watch them leave that way."

"Not as much as it would have hurt to go back to being my father's little puppet. He made every decision for me when I was growing up, including telling me which man to marry. I was suffocating in that life. It all kept building inside me until it finally exploded on my twenty-sixth birthday. I can't live that way anymore."

Trent thought of the money, the security, the social position she'd walked away from. "You gave up a lot."

"I gave up *things*. I found freedom. Of the two, I much prefer the latter."

He nodded thoughtfully. "I can understand that. You must have been slowly suffocating in that household. I'm surprised you didn't bolt long before you did."

"There were so many times I wanted to. But I always let my mother talk me out of it. This time, she didn't even try, not really. Maybe she knew it was inevitable."

"Your father seemed to know a lot about your life here. You think he really was having someone keep an eye on you?"

She bit her lip, looking so distressed by that possibility that he was tempted to go beat someone up again. And then she smoothed her expression and shrugged. "If he was, he'll know now that there's no reason to spy on me any longer. I'm getting along just fine without him—which, of course, infuriates him."

She turned and rested her hands on his chest, looking up at him with suddenly glowing eyes. "Even though I could have handled that scene myself, it was nice to have you here supporting me. Thank you."

He lifted a hand to her cheek and shook his head with a rueful expression. "You're so determined to be self-sufficient that you can't admit that everyone needs help sometimes."

"Even you?" she countered.

"Even me," he surprised them both by answering.

He could see her pulse begin to beat a little faster in the hollow of her throat. His own was suddenly racing. "What do you need now, Trent?"

"You," he answered steadily. "I need *you*, Annie. Not because I can't live without you—but because I don't want to."

Her eyes filled with tears. She rose on tiptoe, her hands clutching his shirt for balance.

His mouth met hers halfway.

THE FIRST TIME Annie and Trent had made love it had been spectacular, but a bit fast—not that Annie had had any complaints. This time, Trent seemed to feel as if he had all the time in the world. To taste. To explore. To tease and tantalize.

There wasn't an inch of her body he missed in his very thorough exploration. Not the smallest patch of skin he didn't kiss. She didn't know if hours passed, or minutes, and she didn't care. She wanted this night to go on forever.

When there was no part of her he hadn't found and

claimed, she returned the favor, urging him onto his back so she could get to know him as intimately as he now knew her. Every muscle, every angle, every scar—there was no part of him she didn't find appealing. Maybe he wasn't perfect—but he was close enough to suit her.

Finally pushed past control, Trent loomed over her again, reaching hastily into the nightstand. He didn't speak when he made love with her—but he had his own way of communicating. He fused their mouths at the same time he joined their bodies, so that nothing separated them, not even a breath of air could come between them. And then he thrust so deeply into her that he became a part of her.

The only sound in the room were gasps and moans and the steady, rhythmic creaking of the secondhand bed, then just ragged, panting breaths as they lay sprawled together in the tangled sheets, trying to regain some semblance of sanity.

After a long time, Trent shifted his weight and pulled Annie more comfortably against him. She felt him wince, then shift again. "Are you all right?" she asked, her voice still husky.

"Yeah. Just a twinge. I can't lie on my side very long."

She'd never heard him sound quite so casual in response to a question about his back. Did he finally understand that she accepted his injuries as a part of him, something to be compensated for and then pretty much forgotten about? Was he finally starting to see them in much the same way?

After a minute, Trent spoke, his voice low. "You

called me a bonus, but I'm not much of a bargain, Annie."

She lifted her head to look at him. "Don't start talking that way again. Don't you know I've never seen you the way you saw yourself?"

"I can't offer you the things your father or that Preston jerk could give you. But you have my respect and my admiration...and my love. Things they didn't seem to know how to offer."

Her throat was so tight it was hard to speak. She lifted a hand to his face, noting again how vulnerable his eyes looked without the barrier of his glasses. "There's nothing more I want. I love you, too, Trent."

He seemed to be holding back, as if he wasn't sure she completely understood him. "You were absolutely right that I won't touch your money. I make my own way—and it'll be a while before my cabinetry business turns much of a profit, if ever."

"You'll make a profit," she predicted happily. "You're too good not to. And I can support myself, remember?"

"I don't like you working so hard," he muttered with a renewed frown. "You're trying to do too much. Maybe you think I'm interfering in your life again, but it's because I care about you, not because I want to control you."

"I know. You're right, Trent, I have been trying to do too much."

He looked a bit suspiciously at her, as if attempting to decide why she'd agreed so easily this time.

She smiled crookedly. "I guess I was trying to prove something to my father—and maybe to myself. Now it's time to decide what I really want to do, rather than what will be the most effective rebellion against my father."

"And what is that?" he asked, lying very still as he studied her face.

"I really don't mind cleaning, but what I really love is teaching. I'd like to use part of my inheritance to buy a piano and set up a studio. The rest I'll invest in case of future emergencies. I won't rival my father's fortune by giving piano lessons, but I think I can make enough to support myself."

"I think you can do anything you want to do."

She beamed at him. "I know. You're the first person who ever believed that about me. Everyone else seems to think I'm helpless, for some reason."

"Anyone who truly believes that about you is a moron."

She placed a hand on either side of his face and kissed him firmly. "Thank you. That's the sweetest thing anyone has ever said to me."

His smile was crookedly resigned. "I guess I'm just a sweet guy."

"Yes," she murmured, snuggling more securely against him. "You most definitely are."

They lay in silence for a few minutes and then Trent spoke again, his tone suspiciously casual. "We could save a little money if we moved in together and maintained one household instead of two."

Her pulse began to race again. "I suppose we could."

"And if we're going to do that, we might as well make it legal."

"Trent, are you asking me to marry you?"

He cleared his throat. "Yeah. I guess I am. I'm probably not doing it right—I'm not very good at that sort of thing. But I love you, and I want us to start our new lives together. I want what Tara and Trevor have found, and I want it with you. If you need more time, it's okay. I just thought you should know it's what I have in mind, so you can be thinking about it."

It wasn't the most romantic proposal she'd ever heard—Trent wasn't the traditionally romantic type. But Annie couldn't imagine it being any more perfect. "I don't have to think about it, Trent. I would love to marry you. There's no one I'd rather start my new life with."

He was beginning to smile now. "Flaws and all?"

She kissed him again. "Flaws and all."

"You'll never be sorry, Annie. I'll make sure of that."

"Oh, Trent. That's so very—"

He pulled her mouth to his quickly, before she could say the word again. But she still thought he was sweet, she thought, sinking happily into his kiss.

Epilogue

THE LIGHTS OF HONORIA, Georgia were reflected in the rearview mirror of his rental car as Mac Cordero left town. He wasn't in the best of moods. He'd made no headway in solving the riddle that had brought him here in the first place. To make it worse, that cleaning woman—Annie Stewart—had twice spotted him watching the McBrides, causing Trent to overreact with some ridiculous idea that he was a stalker or something. Swapping rental cars had allayed Annie's fears, but Mac wasn't sure he had convinced Trent.

He would worry about that complication when he returned at the beginning of June, he decided, pushing the image of Trent's suspicious blue eyes out of his mind. And the next time he came to Honoria, he wouldn't be leaving until he'd accomplished his mission.

The McBride family owed him. Their secrets were about to be revealed.

Don't miss the exciting conclusion to the McBride saga in YESTERDAY'S SCANDAL, a single title release available in September 2000.

If you enjoyed what you just read,
then we've got an offer you can't resist!

Take 2 bestselling love stories FREE!

Plus get a FREE surprise gift!

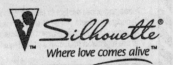

HARLEQUIN
Duets™

HARLEQUIN®
Temptation.

Buckhorn County, Kentucky, may not have any famous natural wonders, but it *does* have the unbeatable Buckhorn Brothers. Doctor, sheriff, heartthrob and vet—all different, all irresistible, all larger than life.

There isn't a woman in town who isn't in awe of at least one of them.

But somehow, they've managed to hang on to their bachelor status. Until now...

Lori Foster presents:

Sawyer
#786, On Sale June 2000

Morgan
#790, On Sale July 2000

Gabe
#794, On Sale August 2000

Jordan
#798, On Sale September 2000

The BUCKHORN BROTHERS

All gorgeous, all sexy, all single. *What a family!*

HT4BROS